"I'm not a sheriff." Not anymore.

He helped her regain her balance on her own two feet, his hand still pressed into her lower back. Bands of heat swirled through her, and she forced herself to step out of his reach. To prove she could. She wasn't a sheriff anymore, and he wasn't a private investigator anymore, but that didn't make the desire bubbling under her skin any more appropriate. She was the chief deputy of this district—his superior. If the top United States marshal himself got even a hint of intimacy between her and Dylan, she'd lose her job and he'd be suspended.

She couldn't let the past ruin what she'd built here. For either of them.

THE SUSPECT

NICHOLE SEVERN

To my mind-blowing readers:

Keep buying my books, please.

But seriously, you're amazing.

Recycling programs for this product may not exist in your area.

ISBN-13: 978-1-335-40167-0

The Suspect

This edition published by arrangement with Harlequin Books S.A.

For questions and comments about the quality of this book, please contact us at CustomerService@Harlequin.com.

Harlequin Enterprises ULC
22 Adelaide St. West, 40th Floor
Toronto, Ontario M5H 4E3, Canada
www.Harlequin.com

Printed in U.S.A.

Nichole Severn writes explosive romantic suspense with strong heroines, heroes who dare challenge them and a hell of a lot of guns. She resides with her very supportive and patient husband, as well as her demon spawn, in Utah. When she's not writing, she's constantly injuring herself running, rock climbing, practicing yoga and snowboarding. She loves hearing from readers through her website, www.nicholesevern.com, and on Twitter, @nicholesevern.

Books by Nichole Severn

Harlequin Intrigue

A Marshal Law Novel

The Fugitive
The Witness
The Prosecutor
The Suspect

Blackhawk Security

Rules in Blackmail
Rules in Rescue
Rules in Deceit
Rules in Defiance
Caught in the Crossfire
The Line of Duty

Midnight Abduction

Visit the Author Profile page at Harlequin.com.

CAST OF CHARACTERS

Remington "Remi" Barton—Small-town sheriff turned chief deputy US marshal. Remi's failure to catch a serial killer from her days as a Delaware sheriff is about to put everything she's tried to protect in danger, including one of her own deputies.

Dylan Cove—As a former private investigator, Dylan is more than capable of uncovering the truth, but his past mistakes threaten to derail the hunt for a killer and compromise his future with Remi.

Beckett Foster—Deputy US marshal assigned out of Oregon division office.

Finnick Reed—Deputy US marshal with specialized experience hunting serial killers assigned out of Oregon division office.

Jonah Watson—Deputy US marshal and former FBI bomb technician assigned out of Oregon division office.

New Castle Killer—Credited with murdering three college-age victims in Delaware, the New Castle Killer is determined to finish what he's started with Remi, but what happens when another killer catches up with this serial killer?

Chapter One

Some people believed evil could be predicted. It couldn't.

Chief Deputy US Marshal Remington "Remi" Barton stepped over the threshold of the small cabin on the outskirts of the city. Sitting between Mount Hood and Portland, Gresham, Oregon, was one of the state's largest cities, but it still hung on to that small-town feel. One hundred thousand people lived within the limits, yet not a single one of them had been close enough to hear the victim scream.

"Heard you might have seen something like this back in Delaware, Chief." Sergeant Daniel Nguyen, the Gresham officer who'd called her to check out the scene, motioned her inside. He flipped open a small notebook and cradled a pencil in his other hand. Handsome Asian heritage highlighted sharp cheekbones, a thin nose and thick black hair. Dark eyes scanned the scene. "The medical examiner is on her way, and the crime scene unit will be finished in a few minutes. No forced entry, and whoever finished the job had wiped down any surfaces before leaving the victim. I doubt we'll be able to pull fingerprints. Whoever did this sure as hell knew how to clean up after themselves."

"You said a pair of hikers found him after one of them got sick and were knocking on doors for help. They saw him through the window?" Dread pooled at the base of her spine. The heavy scent of copper and decomposition twisted Remi's stomach as she cleared the path of a tech leaving the scene. The USMS didn't normally investigate homicide cases. Remi and the team she supervised were specifically trained in fugitive recovery, prisoner transport, asset forfeiture and witness security, but she couldn't ignore the detailed similarities between this victim and the memories she'd run from.

Sergeant Nguyen lifted his pencil from the notebook and motioned with the eraser end toward the back of the cabin. "The body is in the bedroom. They saw it through the window on the south side of the house. I collected statements from both hikers before EMTs took the female hiker—Annabell Ross—to the hospital. Seems she contracted a stomach bug from drinking straight out of a stream near here. The other one, a guy named Henry Sallow, is still here giving his statement.

Neither of them saw or heard anything suspicious, as far as they remember. I pulled the property records and informed the owners about what happened. We don't get a lot of homicides in Gresham. Have you been out here before?"

"No. Most of my cases keep me in Portland." A stone fireplace took up most of the space in the small living room, a kitchen just beyond that to the right at the back of the structure. Shadows cast across the hardwood through the windows from a ring of pines stretching overhead outside. Remi took in the old sofa, a coffee table and the small built-in bookshelves on either side of the fireplace. No personal effects or décor. No television. Not unusual for a place like this in the middle of nowhere. It was hard enough getting electricity let alone cable, but the place looked deserted. A rental? Or an opportunity the killer had taken advantage of?

A mountainous wall of muscle shadowed the doorframe behind her as Deputy US Marshal Dylan Cove stepped onto the scene, and every cell in Remi's body rocketed into awareness. Well over six-two, with healthy, brown hair, a permanent scowl and gray eyes she found herself unable to avoid, the former private investigator locked his attention on her with an intensity that'd followed her all the way from Delaware. "Do we know how long the victim had been staying here?"

"Not yet, but there's an overnight bag in the closet behind you with a few changes of clothes, so I'm thinking he was on vacation." Nguyen leveled his gaze with hers. The glare from the sunlight reflecting off his silver badge prevented her from seeing his expression. Daniel Nguyen had been Gresham police longer than she'd headed her division. He was a veteran, experienced with homicide investigations and evidence collection, and was perfectly capable of handling this scene on his own. What were she and Cove doing there? The sergeant faced her. "Are you sure you've never been here?"

"Positive. We don't get scenes like this in my division." She would've remembered if one of her assignments had brought her out here. The closest she'd come had been to drive straight through Gresham on her way to Mount Hood during a case in which a senior deputy district attorney had been abducted and her team had been called in to provide backup. Her boots reverberated off the hardwood floors as she followed the sergeant toward the back of the cabin. Remi memorized the floor plan as they moved down the short hallway, past the secondary kitchen access and into the northwest corner of the house. The hairs on the back of her neck stood on end as heavy footsteps fell into rhythm behind her. Cove. Wall paneling dimmed the natural light coming in through the single window as she rounded the corner, and there, in the center of the bedroom, was the reason she'd been called to the scene.

Her throat worked to repress the bile churning in her gut. The victim—male, approximately six feet, maybe one hundred and eighty pounds—had been tied to a chair by the wrists and ankles. She zeroed in on the blood crusted under the ropes, evidence the cuts on his skin had more than likely resulted from his spending hours trying to escape. However, it was the dozens of other lacerations, the ones that'd most likely led to his death, that demanded her attention. Her mouth dried as the past collided with the present. Memories of a scene almost identical to this one threatened to escape the grave she'd buried them in when she'd left Delaware. The rope, the lacerations varying in width and length across the victim's entire body, the lack of forced entry and isolated location. "Do you have a pair of gloves for me?"

Nguyen circled around one of the crime scene technicians and collected a pair of latex gloves then handed them off. "We recovered the victim's wallet on the dresser over there. Delaware license belonging to Del Howe. You recognize the name?"

"Should we?" Cove donned his own pair of gloves and flipped open the victim's wallet. He hadn't showed any signs of surprise or recognition since coming into the room. Of all the investigators who'd worked the New Castle Killer case, she would've expected him to react to this scene.

"Doesn't sound familiar." Did Nguyen honestly believe because she and the victim were both from Delaware, she'd know him? Styled dirty-blond hair cascaded over Mr. Howe's forehead, hiding most of his face as his chin rested on his chest. Bands of muscle roped down the victim's arms and across his back, yet there was no sign of a struggle in the cabin. Nothing seemed out of place. "Del Howe obviously worked out, took care of himself. Makes me think he wouldn't have gone down without a fight. His attacker must've been bigger, stronger, or he'd been drugged with a sedative."

She took in the clean floor, the furniture, the rumpled bed—everything seemingly in its place. Centering herself in the door frame, she focused on the bed. "But there aren't any defensive wounds on his hands or skin under his fingernails, as far as I can tell. He could've known his attacker. It's possible he let them in, and whoever killed him took him by surprise."

The sergeant scribbled in his notebook. "We'll know more once the medical examiner has a chance to do the autopsy."

"You obviously connected my last case in Delaware to this one, Sergeant, and I can't lie, there are a lot of similarities." Remi forced herself to take a calming breath, to detach from the case that'd ended her career as the sheriff of New Castle, Delaware, and secured her emotional armor in place. But having Cove here—having another investigator who shouldered as much blame as she did for what'd happened on that case—threatened to resurrect the past. She kept her gaze on the corner of the bed and not on the pool of blood that'd seeped into the cracks of the hardwood floor around the body. "The manner of binding the victim to a chair, the dozens of cuts that most likely caused him to bleed out, the lack of struggle and the fact there are no signs of forced entry."

This scene ticked all the boxes neither she nor Cove had been able to solve. But what were the chances the killer who'd gotten away with three murders of college-aged men back east had come to Oregon?

"Do you believe this could be the work of the New Castle Killer?" Sergeant Nguyen poised his pencil above the notebook that doubled as a barrier between him and the victim. "That he followed you here from Delaware in order to taunt you?"

Cove's head snapped up.

"I'm not ready to make that jump yet, Sergeant." Now why on earth would the sergeant think she was connected to this case at all? There were hundreds of thousands of murders a year in the United States but only so many different ways to kill a human being. There was bound to be some overlap from one case to another. Remi moved around Del Howe's body toward the back of the bedroom. No sign of company while he'd been in Oregon. No female clothing, long hairs on the pillowcases or feminine touches. The crime scene unit would be able to confirm the victim hadn't had any visitors, but the knot in her chest wouldn't let her discount the possibility Nguyen had a point. Of all the locations this killer could've caught up to his prey, why take a cold case she'd worked in New Castle and recreate it here in Gresham? To get her attention? To send a message?

"I'm more inclined to believe whoever did this was a copycat," Cove said. "The investigation got a lot of national attention after the last victim went missing and, no matter how hard we tried to prevent it, the media uncovered a lot of details we never released to the public."

"I'm happy to turn over my case files and notes if you want to compare the scenes." Anything to dislodge the knot of guilt twisting in her gut. She hadn't been able to bring any of the victims home, but there might be something in her old files that could help Gresham PD prevent it from happening again. A soft click registered from the corner of the large bedroom, and Remi realized the crime scene photographer was documenting everything inside the walk-in closet.

Confusion rippled up her neck and across her

shoulders as something compelled her to look inside. Had there been more blood evidence found in the closet? She forced one foot in front of the other as the crime scene photographer angled his camera at the floor, backing out of her way as he studied the LCD screen on his camera.

Revealing the surveillance photos taped over every square inch of the closet.

Remi froze as recognition flared.

It was her. The photo to her left showed her crossing the office parking lot. Then, straight ahead, one of her coordinating a manhunt at Heceta Head Lighthouse when a serial killer had taken one of her marshal's witnesses. To her right, the photo was of her debriefing the firefighters at the scene of a thermite bomb explosion. Every photo was of her. Hundreds of them.

She didn't understand, turning to Cove in a desperate attempt to make sense of what the surveillance meant. This was why Gresham PD had pulled her into the investigation.

Nguyen stepped up behind her as the world threatened to rip straight out from under her. "You can see why we might've wanted to question you concerning the murder of Del Howe, Chief Deputy Barton."

GRESHAM PD WASN'T going to pin this on Remi.

Deputy US Marshal Dylan Cove pushed into the

police station. Battle-ready tension tightened the muscles down his spine as he scanned the folding chairs directly ahead of him then the long desk with a single officer on the other side. Remi wasn't there. The sergeant who'd been at the scene hadn't put her under arrest, but Dylan had read the officer's desperation to connect Remi to the scene through the discovery of those surveillance photos.

Most of Gresham's crime fell into domestic and burglary offenses. The local police didn't have a whole lot of experience with a murder investigation, but when they had one, they wanted it handled quietly. With only one hundred thousand or so residents, Gresham, Oregon, tried to hold on to a small-town feel while growing every year. That meant keeping the news of a victim viciously murdered in a cabin outside the city limits under wraps and solving the investigation as quickly as possible to prevent panic.

And those photos of Remi… Dylan curled his fingers into fists as he pushed past the front desk and stalked toward the back of the station. They'd done their job in giving the chief deputy motive for killing the victim. A humorless scoff escaped his throat. The victim.

Del Howe wasn't a victim.

The SOB had gotten exactly what he'd deserved.

Rows of empty desks bled into Dylan's peripheral vision as he focused on the single conference room at the rear of the station. A head of long black hair materialized through the barrier of white plastic blinds, and every sense he owned homed in on her. Remi. Rage coiled tight as he watched her square off with Captain Elijah Paulson. A dense gray beard hid the length of the captain's neck as he pushed a single photo from the crime scene across the conference table. The captain's blue eyes, almost as colorless as Remi's, narrowed on his chief and spiked Dylan's blood pressure. He put the captain mid-fifties, early sixties, but Elijah Paulson was far from retirement. Mentally and physically.

Remi's team had only one other case Dylan could recall that had brought them into the captain's radar, but that short amount of time had been all Dylan had needed to get a read on the man himself. Intense, reliable, hardworking. Exactly what Gresham deserved from a police captain. Someone who dedicated himself to the job to serve the citizens of the town and not to inflate an oversize ego. Of all the officers in Gresham, Dylan trusted Paulson to see past the sergeant's mistake in bringing Remi in and to treat Del Howe as the psychopath he was—had been. Not a victim.

His heart thundered behind his ears, an uneasy rhythm as he sat on the edge of the desk behind him and waited. Remi didn't need him to burst in there and save her. The chief deputy was one of the most self-reliant, straight-talking women he'd ever known. She could handle herself.

Remi pushed back in her seat to stand and turn toward the door. Iridescent blue eyes settled on him as she reached for the handle and wrenched it open. Every cell in his body responded to her as he straightened.

She'd shut down her expression, but Dylan had known Remi long enough to read past that controlled facade. That meeting might've revealed her alibi at the time of Del Howe's death, but it would certainly raise more questions.

She closed the conference room door behind her. The green cargo pants and skintight long-sleeved running shirt highlighted the brightness of her eyes and the sharp angles of her cheekbones. "Any other photos I need to know about back at the scene? Maybe something showing I was the one who tied Del Howe to a chair and cut him repeatedly until he bled out. Because being a stranger's obsession doesn't quite feel good enough."

"Went that well, huh?" He held back his smile as sarcasm dripped from her perfectly shaped mouth. "I had CSU take me through the rest of the scene, inside and out. No such photos. The only vehicle tracks leading up to the cabin belong to the rental Howe paid for three days ago, and the techs haven't been able to put anyone else there at the time of the murder."

Yet.

"Well, the victim didn't do this to himself." Remi surveyed the rest of the station before resting that startling gaze on him. She stepped into him and lowered her voice, and his insides clenched. "You saw the way he was butchered, Cove. I know you're thinking the same thing as I am. Delaware driver's license, same MO as the New Castle Killer. This victim is a few years older than the first three, but what are the chances these cases aren't connected? We never caught up with him."

Cove. She'd gone back to using his last name the moment they'd stopped sleeping together after she'd taken up with the marshals service and left him behind. Dylan pulled back his shoulders, trying to offset the lingering desire constantly coiled in his gut when she got this close. "You think the killer followed his prey here."

Not just any prey. Her. The surveillance photos had exposed Remi as a target.

"We were close. We almost had him after the third victim disappeared, but I..." She'd lost her elected position as New Castle County's sheriff for failing to capture a killer determined to stay two steps ahead of them. She'd been forced to step away from the case and shamed by the public for not being able to get the job done. Remi didn't have to say the words. He knew. She'd been the one to bring him onto the case when the department had exhausted all the county's resources and manpower, and he'd been shut out the moment the people had removed her from office. "This feels like him. Like he wants to finish the game he started. I don't know how he found us, but it's not over. Not for him."

Dylan caught sight of an empty office at the other end of the station. Threading his hand between her rib cage and arm, he directed her through the maze of desks and unanswered phones. "Come with me."

"What are you doing?" Lean muscle strained against the inside of his hand, but Remi didn't move to wrench out of his hold altogether.

He swung her ahead of him and followed close on her heels into the darkened space. She turned on him as he closed the door, the fluorescent light coming through the blinds carving shadows into her features. Hints of her citrus scent tickled the back of his throat as he closed the distance between them, and he breathed in as much as his lungs allowed to counter the sickening nausea behind the truth. No one would overhear them here. "I knew Del Howe was here."

"You knew the victim." Her eyebrows drew inward, deepening the lines between them, then smoothed. Cocking her head to one side, Remi studied his face from forehead to chin, every inch the former sheriff he remembered. Uncompromising. Strong. One of the first things he'd noticed about her when she'd hired him to work the New Castle Killer case had been her unending patience while she waited for her suspects to fill the silence. She'd done a damn fine job as sheriff. Not a whole lot had changed between that investigator he'd met and the chief deputy standing in front of him. If anything, she'd only impressed him more.

"We weren't friends." Hard to be friends with someone he'd surveilled from a safe distance for over a year. Nervous energy shot down his fingers. Del Howe had been alive the last time Dylan had seen him. One piece of hair, one tread from his boot—that was all it would take to swing this investigation in the wrong direction. He had to get out in front of this while he still could. "But it's possible my DNA might be recovered at the cabin where Del Howe was killed."

Her exhale brushed against the underside of his chin and heightened his awareness of how close she'd let him get. Folding her arms across her chest, Remi shifted her weight between both feet before her expression collapsed with understanding. "You mean other than the fact you were there to walk the scene less than an hour ago."

"I warned the owners what kind of man they'd let stay in their rental. They were only too happy to give me a key to the place to make sure nothing had gone missing or that he wasn't doing anything illegal. I waited until Howe drove down the mountain before I went inside. I swear. He was alive when I left. I didn't kill him." Would she believe him? He pulled back his shoulders. "I was searching for proof he was the man I've been looking for, and when I saw the photos of you in the closet, I knew I had the right guy."

"What do you mean what kind of man they let stay there?" Remi unfolded her arms and stepped closer to him. Scanning the station on the other side of the window, she lowered her voice so as not to divert Captain Paulson or any other officers' attention their way. "Who is Del Howe, and what does any of this have to do with those surveillance photos of me?"

"I first caught on to him in Delaware. I had reason to believe he'd kill, so I've been investigating him in my free time. Small stuff at first. I had a PI friend in New Castle run a background check then I cashed in a favor from the DA to put a tail on him."

Dylan prepared for the coming lecture from his superior. He'd been running an investigation behind his chief's back, using his position as a marshal without jurisdiction. Any evidence he'd collected against Del Howe wouldn't have stood up in court, but Dylan couldn't let the bastard get away. Not again. "Highway Patrol reported he'd crossed into Oregon three days ago."

"What the hell are you talking about?" Her lips parted, homing his gaze to that full mouth he hadn't been able to get out of his mind all these years. Remi turned away from him, a humorless laugh rising up her throat. Ice-blue eyes settled on him. "Why go to all this effort behind my back and not brief me on the details before he became the subject of a murder investigation? What did you suspect Del Howe was guilty of before he was killed?"

"I wasn't going to let him get to you, Sheriff." In truth, past anger and guilt had driven him to this moment, but he wasn't going to apologize for keeping her safe. No matter how much distance she'd physically and emotionally put between them.

"Me? I've never met that man before in my life," she said. "Why would he have reason to target me?"

Dylan forced himself to keep the aggression out of his voice. "Because Del Howe is—was—the New Castle Killer."

Chapter Two

Del Howe was the killer who'd gotten away.

How was that possible? Remi stepped out of Dylan's reach. She'd worked that case for a full year before the people had decided the town needed a new investigator on the case, and not once had a suspect fitting Del Howe's name or description come across her desk. "We had solid suspects we looked into on that case. None of them Del Howe. How can you be sure the victim Gresham PD discovered this morning is the New Castle Killer?"

"You mean apart from the fact the guy followed you here all the way from Delaware, had surveillance photos of you taped to the inside of his closet and was murdered with the same MO the New Castle Killer used?" Dark hair caught the dim lighting coming through the blinds. With his face partially in shadow, she didn't have to see his expression to read how hard it was for Dylan to keep the lid on all that rage and guilt. He blamed himself for the deaths of those three young men, and, in a sense, he was right. If the former private investigator had taken the third victim's concern for his safety seriously, Dylan probably could've gotten to him before the New Castle Killer had. They'd never found his remains, but evidence at the scene had confirmed Tad Marrow had been bound, cut and murdered by the killer they'd been trying to stop.

Dylan unpocketed his phone, the light from the screen failing to chase back the haunted shadows etched into his features. He handed her the device and swiped through a series of photos dated over a year ago. "The buildings where all three victims lived in Delaware were inspected by the same man around the time of each of their deaths."

"Del Howe?" The signature was clear. How many times had she gone through those files only to end right back where she'd started: without motive or a viable suspect. Too many. That was why the people had forced her to step down as sheriff. She'd failed to protect her county. But where Remi had left the past behind after being removed from her position, Dylan had ignored the her orders to back down. He'd taken up the investigation himself, even after all this time, and made a solid connection between the victims they hadn't been able to before. "You made the connection after we were banned from investigating the case, and you didn't want to incriminate me if you were caught."

Of course he had. Because that was the kind of man Dylan Cove was, the kind to think about the consequences of his actions and how those same actions would affect everyone in his life. The kind to never give up, to complete his mission, to do whatever it took to solve the case. It was what had made him a great private investigator and one of the reasons she'd hired him to help her work the New Castle Killer case.

It was his dedication to the job that had caught her attention and had led to the most passionate weeks of her life. Then it had all come to an abrupt halt.

After the people had publicly called for her resignation, she hadn't been able to face him, to bear the weight of her failure to protect her county. So she'd left. She'd taken a job with the US Marshals Service, worked to forget her previous life and risen up the ranks until she'd been assigned to head up the Oregon division. Ending their relationship—or whatever it'd been between them—had just been part of starting over.

Until he'd walked into her office six months ago, asking her to help him make up for letting a killer slip through their fingers. He was a good marshal but an even better investigator, and she would need his help to prove she wasn't the one who'd killed Del Howe.

"You were starting over here. You had a good thing going. I didn't want to be the one to screw that up." Dylan followed her retreat, closing the small space between them, and the hairs on the back of her neck stood at attention. He'd always had that effect on her, always keeping her off-balance and grounded at the same time, and she didn't know what to do about it other than to pretend he didn't have this hold on her.

Of all the people she'd kept at a professional distance, he'd blown past her guard, gotten under her skin, made her believe she could be more than the washed-up sheriff who'd let a killer get away. He slid his hands up her arms, hiking the cuffs of her sleeves higher, and studied the designs peeking out from underneath.

Tattoos. Three names of the victims she hadn't been able to help inked in block letters. Part of her. She'd had an appointment to have the names removed when she'd come to Oregon, but the need to remember her failure had been too strong.

Smoothing his thumb along her inner wrist, Dylan brought that mesmerizing gray gaze to hers. "I know why you left, Remi. Hell, I don't even blame you for not telling me before you took the job with USMS, but I knew it wasn't over. Not for him."

A trail of sensation burned up her arms, but as much as she wanted to lean into it, to remember what it'd felt like to drown the nightmares that had followed her from Delaware, there was a killer outside these walls. Waiting.

Remi shrugged out of his reach. "I can think of any number of people who'd have motive to want the New Castle Killer dead, but they would've had to know who he really was. They would've had to connect the elevator inspections to the victims' abduction dates, same as you. Did you tell anyone about Del Howe? About who he really was?"

"No. Like I said, I didn't want any part of my personal investigation to come back on you or anyone else in the division." He spread his fingers wide at his sides, a glimmer of disappointment in his eyes.

Or was that her imagination?

"We never released the details of how the New Castle Killer tortured and killed his victims to the media during the investigation, but that didn't stop some of them from leaking. Whoever came for Del Howe had intimate knowledge of the crime and knew where to find him." She had to think this through. Because despite the theory that Del Howe had been in all three buildings around the same time each victim disappeared, it wasn't proof the man in the cabin had been the New Castle Killer. The only way to get that would be to dig back into the files. Her stomach revolted. "I believe you when you say you didn't kill him, but I need to know if there is anything else you're keeping from me."

Tension flared across his shoulders and up through the tendons in Dylan's neck. A hint of hesitation chased back the disappointment that with her next breath had vanished. Another trick of the shadows? "I've told you everything. I got rid of my vehicle's tracks when I headed back down the mountain after searching the cabin two days ago, but there's still a chance CSU can place me inside. DA Madison Gray will be able to confirm my call to ask for her help, and the cabin's owners can tell you I had their permission to search the premises."

"I'll call Madison and the homeowners to confirm in order to eliminate you as a suspect, but you'll need to give your statement and an alibi for the timeframe Del Howe was murdered." Hands on her hips, she scanned the movements of the officers on the other side of the window. An itch climbed up her spine. No matter how much she wanted to forget her years on the force, there was a part of her that'd missed it. A strong exhale escaped up her throat. "Gresham PD has jurisdiction over this case. Once we have signed statements from the DA and the cabin's owners, you'll turn everything you have on Del Howe over to Captain

Paulson and let them do their jobs. Understood?" Remi maneuvered around him and headed for the office door.

"You can't keep running, Remi." His voice penetrated through the slight ringing in her ears and notched her blood pressure higher. His heavy footsteps closed in on her from behind and forced her hand to tighten around the doorknob. "We're the ones who made this mess. We're the ones who let the New Castle Killer slip away. Don't you think we owe it to his victims to see this through? That we share just as much of the responsibility to keep his sickness from spreading?"

The empty space she let her mind retreat into when the past caught up threatened to swallow her whole. Her pulse ticked at the base of her throat as images of the crime scenes surfaced.

"Del Howe had photos of me taped all over the inside of his closet, Dylan. That, in and of itself, gives me motive for wanting to confront him from the captain's point of view. Sergeant Nguyen as much as accused me of somehow finding out I was being stalked and killing the man myself while I was in that conference room, and you're telling me Del Howe is the killer that ended my career. The only way I was able to leave that room not in cuffs was to give him an alibi at the time of Del Howe's death."

She turned toward him, her hand slipping from

the doorknob. "And you admitted to being at that cabin two days before the victim was found dead by those hikers. If forensics turns up any evidence that you were there, Gresham PD will arrest you. You know as well as I do we won't be allowed anywhere near this case as long as we're considered suspects."

Dylan crossed the small office, and her body instantly heated. "Who said anything about working this case officially?"

Her breath hitched. He wanted to continue his unofficial investigation of Del Howe. "You're asking your chief deputy to turn a blind eye?"

"I'm asking you to trust me like you did in Delaware, Sheriff." His voice dropped into dangerous territory, eliciting a vibration deep in her belly. In the six months Dylan Cove had worked in her division, not once had he asked her for a favor or used their past against her. He'd respected her need to leave the nightmares behind and let her move on with her life. Until now. "Let me do this. Let me prove Del Howe was the New Castle Killer. Let me give his victims' families the answers they've been waiting for and keep another killer from getting away with murder. Please."

Her heart jerked in her chest. He'd made a mistake on the New Castle Killer case. This was his attempt to make up for it. Remi directed her gaze out the cutout window of the office door and located Captain Paulson exiting the conference room with the same crime scene photos he'd slid across the table toward her a few minutes before. She recognized Paulson for the man he was: proud, self-serving, controlling. Even if she cleared her and Dylan as suspects, he wouldn't let two US marshals near his investigation unless forced, but arrogance had no place in a case like this. If the killer who'd caught up to Del Howe was willing to bleed a victim to death for revenge, there was no telling how far he'd go the next time. "We're going to need some help."

THE OREGON DISTRICT office of the United States Marshals Service buzzed with printers and ringing phones from the other side of the conference room glass, but Dylan only had attention for the men and women positioned around the table. He pressed his elbows into the reflective oak surface.

"You're all here because I need your help." Remi distributed manila file folders to each participant. Files that contained her old notes and crime scene photos of the Delaware scenes and the background information tied to all three of the New Castle Killer's victims. Tony Rasmussen, Brett Smith and Tad Marrow. "A body was recently discovered in a cabin a quarter mile outside of Gresham's city limits. The victim had been bound to a chair with rope, presumably sedated and cut more than a hundred times over every inch of his body until he bled out.

"Deputy Cove and I believe it has something to do with a case we worked together back in Delaware of a serial killer who murdered three victims in the same manner. We never caught the New Castle Killer nor were we able to identify him before we were taken off the investigation."

"Wouldn't be the first time a serial has crossed state lines." Deputy US Marshal Finnick Reed opened the file folder and skimmed through the crime scene reports. Of the five marshals that worked out of this office, Reed had acquired more experience with serials than anyone on the team after the most notorious killer in Chicago—The Carver—had followed Reed's witness to Oregon. Only now, the psychopath was under six feet of dirt and Reed and his witness were on their way to matrimony.

"You're right. There's just one problem with that assumption." Remi pressed the remote in her hand and brought the projector connected to her laptop to life. A large image of Del Howe, after he'd been killed, took up most of the wall at the head of the conference room, a photo she'd taken with her own phone. "We believe the victim discovered by hikers this morning was the New Castle Killer."

A low whistle broke through the silence. Deputy Jonah Watson hiked himself closer to the edge of the table and waded through the stack of photos from the scene. The former FBI hazardous devices technician studied the file in front of him, trained to take the smallest piece of evidence and compile a theory on how it got there. But this case was bigger than any of them. Hell, it was bigger than the former Portland district attorney who'd targeted the mother of Watson's son so he could prosecute the Rip City Bomber case himself, but Madison Gray had survived. And won the votes to become the next DA. "Someone killed your serial killer."

"In order for that to happen, the killer would've had to have known the identity of the New Castle Killer and hunted him down." Hinges protested as Beckett Foster, the deputy US Marshal responsible for over half of the fugitive recoveries in the state of Oregon alone, leaned back in his chair. "From the evidence in these files, it looks like neither you nor anyone who worked the case back east was able to get a positive ID on the killer. There was even a theory the murders weren't connected because the last two victims had never been recovered. Says here all you had was one body and three crime scenes with a lot of blood left behind. What makes you think Del Howe is the New Castle Killer?"

Dylan nodded to Remi, who hit the projector button to switch to the next slide. "All three victims lived in apartment buildings with elevators.

All three elevators were inspected by Del Howe within a month of each victim disappearing." A still frame of Del Howe filled the projector screen, the footage taken from a camera angled high above the suspect's head. "I called in a favor and had this this footage pulled from the elevator camera in the second victim's building last week. It's dated eight days before Brett Smith went missing."

Remi clicked to the next slide. "This is from Tony Rasmussen's building three weeks before the first victim disappeared. And this one—" she landed on the last slide "—is from Tad Marrow's building three days before his roommate called police. All show Del Howe in and around the locations where the New Castle Killer's victims were killed and drained of blood."

"Why do serials always go for the blade, huh?" Reed asked.

The chief set the remote on the conference table and weighed both palms against the glossy surface. A haunted exhaustion had thinned the skin and accentuated the dark circles under her eyes, and Dylan clenched his teeth to keep himself from reaching out for her. Remi wouldn't appreciate it. Especially not in a room full of the men she supervised. "We believe someone made the same connection Deputy Cove did then followed Del Howe here to get their revenge."

"You said only the first victim, Tony Rasmussen, was recovered. Police found little else but pools of blood at the other two." Finn Reed domed one hand on the conference table surface. "His Delaware driver's license puts him at five-nine and one hundred and seventy pounds, and this footage only shows Howe carrying a tool bag to do his inspections. How did he get two grown men out of the building on his own?"

"We don't know." Dylan twisted in his chair, facing the other three deputies at the opposite end of the table. "What we need to focus on is the fact that someone figured out who he was and killed him with what looks like the same MO as he murdered his victims—and they might not be finished."

"His moniker is the New Castle Killer." Jonah Watson raised his gaze to Remi's. "He killed all three victims in Delaware. What the hell was he doing here, and why are we the ones looking into a homicide? Murder falls under police jurisdiction, even if you were the original investigator on the case."

"You're right. Marshals have no jurisdiction in a homicide, but it's more complicated than me trying to solve the case that lost me my job as New Castle's sheriff." Remi pulled back her shoulders, and Dylan acknowledged the same tension flooding down his spine. She'd kept her past to herself, kept the truth from the marshals under her purview, but she couldn't ignore it any longer. Neither of them could. "Gresham PD called me this morning once they recognized similarities of this scene to the New Castle murders and asked me to walk the scene. Not only had Del Howe been killed in the same manner as the three victims of the New Castle Killer, but there's evidence that shows Del Howe had been surveilling me for quite some time."

The tendons in Dylan's neck corded tight. "Gresham PD thinks the fact their victim died with hundreds of photos of a US marshal taped to the inside of his closet, that she directly—or indirectly—has something to do with his death. We turned everything we had over to the captain there before we left the station, including the connection between Howe and his victims. His current theory is Remi has been investigating Del Howe on her own all this time, discovered he'd been following her and made sure it never happened again. He wants to pin Howe's death on her, and they won't stop until they do."

"You've got to be kidding me." Becket Foster scrubbed a hand through his thick beard. The brand-new father and husband to a former fugitive crossed his arms over his muscled chest. "You were taken off the force and off the case before you came to work with the marshals, but I have to ask, have you been investigating this case since you left?"

"No, and I have an alibi for the timeframe the medical examiner reports Howe was murdered, thanks to the cameras in this office." Remi took her seat at the head of the table. "As far as I was concerned, the New Castle Killer case was in the past. Until this morning."

"I've been investigating it." The attention of the three marshals weighed heavily on his chest, but he couldn't hide behind Remi's connection any longer. Not if he wanted this team's help to find their latest killer. "Remi hired me as a private investigator in Delaware to work the case alongside New Castle Sheriff's Department. When she was banned from investigating, I was officially taken off the case, too."

"And unofficially?" Jonah Watson asked.

"I wasn't going to let the New Castle Killer get away with what he'd done, considering it was my fault Tad Marrow ended up a victim in the first place." Guilt stole his concentration as memories battled to escape. Dylan focused on the documents in the file in front of him, not seeing anything specific. "He came to me, said he felt like he was being watched and asked if I'd look into it. I was so wrapped up in the New Castle Killer case, I brushed him off. Turned out, he was right."

"Now you think someone uncovered the New

Castle Killer's identity and is out for revenge." Finnick Reed hunched over the crime scene photos. "Del Howe obviously came to Oregon for you, Remi. Barring the possibility you or Cove is the killer and you're keeping that bit of information to yourself, we're looking at victims' family members, possibly another investigator on the case who feels as guilty as you do or another serial who isn't too keen on sharing his territory. The Carver didn't take too kindly to his protégé going after Camille. Turns out, serial killers can get very territorial over their prey."

Hell, Cove hadn't even thought of that. Another killer? His gaze slid to Remi, and the edges of his vision blurred. If Del Howe hadn't been killed in that cabin last night, would he have come for Remi next? Would Dylan have found her in the middle of her office or her house tied to a chair, her skin sliced more than a hundred times? Numbness coursed through him at the thought of losing her as the anchor who'd kept him from going too far with his private investigation into Howe, who'd been his lifeline to keeping him on this side of the law.

"What do you need from us, Chief?" Beckett Foster asked.

Dylan studied the faces looking up at their chief with nothing but drive and determination. All three of these men had battled against their greatest fears and death to protect the people they cared about. Beckett with his fugitive, Finnick with his witness, Jonah with his prosecutor. He focused on the hard bite of Remi's nails into the surface of the table then studied the curve of her cheekbones. Dylan would do the same.

"Should be simple enough. We're going to find a killer. Beckett, look into the victims' family members. I want to know if any of them is in or around Oregon. Jonah, I need you to poke around the personnel files for officers who worked the original investigation from the New Castle Sheriff's Department. See if any of them might still be digging into the case. Finn, you and Camille have the most experience with serials in this area. You're going hunting." Camille, the witness the serial from Chicago had targeted for over a year after he failed to kill her outright.

Remi rested her right hand on her sidearm and the other on her opposite hip, every inch the leader Dylan had come to respect these past few years. "This is an unofficial investigation. Everything we do here has to be off the books. That means no USMS resources and nothing available digitally. We're going old school, and what we find stays between us. If Gresham PD gets the smallest hunch we're working this case, there will be hell to pay. Everything comes through me." She nodded at Dylan. "And nobody makes a mistake."

Chapter Three

Remi punched the six-digit code into the keypad beside the dead bolt and waited for the lock to disengage. A long driveway disappeared to the back of the safe house, four light-stained pillars standing guard at her back. The property had been part of an ongoing case in which the owner had lost her home and the surrounding land due to her involvement with prostitution and illegal immigration.

Nobody would be looking for her here.

Her boots echoed off the tile of the grand entryway as she turned to secure the dead bolt. To her left, a two-storied living space climbed high overhead; to the right, a small office she never intended to use. Too exposed with the large front window overlooking the wraparound porch and street. Remi rounded into the main room and pulled the cord to the right of the windows to cut off the view from the street. She couldn't go back to her apartment. Despite the fact Del Howe—the man who'd been surveilling her—had been found dead, there was a chance the person who'd killed him was connected to the New Castle Killer case. What better way to satisfy a craving for revenge than to target the former sheriff who'd let the killer slip away?

Movement registered from the other side of the window a split second before three knocks filled the entryway, and she reached for her sidearm. "I know you're in there, Sheriff. I might not be a private investigator anymore, but that doesn't mean I've forgotten how to tail someone without them noticing."

Dylan Cove. She held her breath. Hand still poised over her weapon, she rounded back into the entryway and pressed her free hand against the door. He wasn't supposed to be here. "What are you doing here, Cove?"

"Did you really think I was going to let you take on whoever killed Del Howe alone?" he asked.

How had he…? Three breaths. Four. She unlocked and opened the door. Centered in the frame, Dylan's features demanded every cell in her body to rise to attention. A flood of appreciation charged through her, and Remi tightened her grip on the doorknob. "You followed me because you think I can't take care of myself."

"Hell, no. I followed you because I didn't want to miss the show when you caught up with the perp who took out the New Castle Killer." His laugh rumbled from low in his chest and chased back the defensiveness tightened the muscles down her spine.

Dylan raised the black duffel bag at his side into her peripheral vision. An overnight bag? Exactly how long did he intend on staying here? "Can I come in? You haven't eaten all day, as far as I could tell, so I brought you your favorite. Peanut butter and jelly sandwiches with nacho chips crushed in the middle, and light beer."

Her stomach growled and Remi stepped back to open the door wider. "You know damn well I can't say no to free food."

"That's what I was counting on." That same laugh she'd battled to forget over the past year dove past her defenses and exploded in her belly. No matter the case, no matter the weight that came with hunting a killer and not being able to bring the victims justice, she'd relied on that laugh to get her through the hardest parts. And here they were again, working a case together in an effort to prevent the loss of more innocent lives. "Nice place. Asset forfeiture?"

She secured the door behind him and armed the alarm installed on the nearest wall. "Watson and Reed confiscated it during an investigation two weeks ago. The case is still with the courts and officially assigned to them. No one should have a reason to look for me here."

"Good a safe house as any. At least until we figure out who the hell wanted the man stalking you dead." Dylan slipped the duffel strap from his shoulder. He tipped his head back as he took in the height of the ceilings, the stone fireplace climbing up toward the second floor, the built-in bookcases against one wall. Muscle and tendon flexed and dipped along his shoulders with the slightest movement, and Remi found herself unable to look away. Until he turned piercing gray eyes on her. His gaze lowered to her hand still resting against the butt of her weapon then shot back to hers. "Tell me what's going through your head."

She forced herself to relax and release her grip on her sidearm. "That you didn't come all the way out here to make sure I got something to eat, Cove."

"I hate when you call me that." He dropped the duffel bag at his feet and took a single step toward her. Her heart rate notched higher as he slowly closed the distance between them, her skin on fire under his assessment, but she wouldn't back down. Not from him. "I remember a time when we called each other by our first names, when it was just us, no one else around. I remember how you said my name in the dark."

Heat stirred in her gut. Remi swallowed around the thickness in her throat, determined not to let the memories escape. Because once she let them free, she feared they might never fit back in the recesses she'd buried them in at the back of her mind. She and Cove had been involved while they'd worked the New Castle Killer case, but they'd agreed it'd been nothing more than a way to slay the nightmares closing in around them, to feel something other than the bottomless disappointment of failure. "That was a long time ago."

"Not for me." He shook his head, the sight of all that brown hair beckoning her fingers to slide through one more time. "Seems like yesterday we were standing face-to-face like we are now in the middle of your office in New Castle after everyone else had been dispatched to an emergency call. The case had beaten us both down to nothing and all we'd had then was each other. Then one day, you were just…gone."

"Is that why you're here?" Hollowness infused her words as he insisted on battering against the invisible barrier she'd constructed to move on with her life. She curled her hands into fists. He'd gotten too close. She wouldn't let him see them shake, wouldn't let him see her break. "You've been working in my office for six months, doing the job, giving me my space, and now, with Del Howe's true identity out in the open, you suddenly have the inclination to bring up a past I'd rather forget. Is that why you joined the marshals after you closed down your private investigation firm? For an apology?"

"I came here because I was worried about you, damn it. I know how you get when you're in the middle of a case. I know you won't eat, you won't sleep and you won't stop until there's nothing left of you to give. You'll blame yourself, and I'm here to tell you you're not the only one who feels responsible for what happened in New Castle. You say you want to forget the past, but I know you, Sheriff." His voice softened. "You won't let the team see anything but the mask you wear day in and day out, but you don't have to do that with me. I've seen the real you. I've seen you at your best and your worst. I know you're hurting and angry, and you're determined to carry the entire division alone, but you're not alone. The sandwiches and beer were just a bribe to get past the front door."

"Well, it worked." He was right. She did blame herself. She'd failed to bring a killer to justice as a sheriff and now, faced with the consequences of that failure, she feared she wasn't strong enough to see this through as a marshal. She hadn't been able to save the victims of the New Castle Killer then. What made her think this time would be any different? And if she failed, would she lose her job as chief deputy, too? "Did you at least use the grape jelly I like?"

"Of course, I did." Dylan stepped back, reached

for the duffel bag he'd set on the floor and retrieved two bagged sandwiches and a couple of longnecks. He handed her one of each and kept the others for himself. "Took my looking in three different stores to find your favorite brand, so when I found it, I bought extra."

He'd done this for her? The bread collapsed under the press of her thumb through the plastic, and her mouth watered. Peanut butter, grape jelly and nacho chips. The meal that'd gotten her through some of the worst moments of her life after her dad had died. But Dylan couldn't have known that. He'd simply picked up on her preferred meal back in Delaware, and she'd never been so thankful for his observation skills than right now. The automatic tightness in her chest when he'd gotten near eased. She led him to the dining table in the next room. Turning on the light, she tamped down her anxiety of being exposed by the wall of floor-to-ceiling glass windows and stay in the moment. She pulled one chair out for him then took her own seat across the table. "Thank you."

"Anytime." He spoke around a mouthful of chips and peanut butter, and she couldn't help but smile at the disgusted look on his face. Dylan set the sandwich on top of the bag he'd wrapped it in and leaned back in his chair. "You eat this every day?"

"It's not that bad." Remi took a bite from her

own sandwich and instantly fell into an emotional safety zone as cheesy nacho chips combined with the sweetness of the grape jelly. “We didn’t have a whole lot of money back in Delaware when I was a kid. Bread, peanut butter, jelly and chips were about as good as it got. My dad used to make this for me every day when I came home from school. Sometimes he used potato chips, but the best are nacho cheese, in my opinion.”

“You never told me about your family.” Dylan tried another bite, but she got the sense he’d only done it to prove he could.

“There’s not a whole lot to tell.” Peanut butter and bread stuck to the roof of her mouth as she focused on the pattern of tree rings engrained into the dining table. She raised her gaze to his. “They’re all dead.”

HELL. SHE’D KEPT such a tight lid on anything having to do with her family, he hadn’t realized it’d been because she didn’t have any left. “I’m sorry. I didn’t know.”

“Nobody knows. The fire happened such a long time ago, I wonder if the memories I have of my parents and my little sister are even real.” Remi traced the zipper along the plastic sandwich bag with her thumb. Her ribs expanded on a strong inhale, and she wrapped both hands around her sandwich as if clinging to it for dear life.

"I was eight. The smoke detector batteries in our trailer had died the week before, but my dad couldn't justify spending what little money we had buying new ones. He'd dedicated his entire life to working in the mines, but almost anyone who hauled coal barely walked away with a living wage. My mom, dad and two-year-old sister were sleeping in the only bed at one end of the trailer with me at the other in a pullout. The last thing I remember was trying to wake them up, but the smoke had already suffocated them. I got my sister out on my own, but even after the paramedics had gotten there, she never woke up."

Remi brushed her hands together to dislodge the crumbs from her fingers, but she still wouldn't look at him. "My parents were too heavy for me to carry by myself. I just...wasn't strong enough. The fire marshal who'd come to investigate said the fire had started because of a faulty outlet in the bedroom. The whole trailer had gone up in a matter of minutes."

"Sounds like you were lucky to get out of there alive," he said.

"I haven't told anyone that story." She shook her head. Remi finished the last of her sandwich, and a new appreciation for the trust she'd showed him spread. She ran a hand through her long black hair and a memory of that same hair surrounding his face as she kissed him surfaced. "Not sure why I told you that, to be honest. I must be more tired than I thought."

"Neither of us was expecting the New Castle Killer case to come back to haunt us after you were let go from the sheriff's department." Dylan played with the crust of his sandwich.

"You believe Del Howe is the killer who outsmarted us all?" That iridescent blue gaze lifted to his, and the world threatened to tip on its axis. He'd known Remi long enough to realize the question went deeper than the words that'd fallen from her lips.

She'd brought him onto the New Castle case based off his previous work as a private investigator. She'd witnessed how far he'd go to get to the truth and had sought him out to work the investigation in tandem with the sheriff's department, despite the blowback from fellow officers and the governor. She wasn't asking him if he was sure he'd uncovered the New Castle Killer's identity. She already knew the truth. No. Remi was asking if he was prepared to step into the ring again, if he was ready to see this case through to the end.

Dylan peeled the corner of the label from his beer as a heavy knot of determination twisted in his gut. "I believe the fact I ignored Tad Marrow when he approached me for help was what got him killed." He took a sip of the beer, not really tasting the flavor as it prickled down the back of his throat. "I promised myself I was going to spend the rest of my life making up for that mistake by ensuring his killer paid for what he'd done. But then the SOB turned up dead this morning. Now I'm not sure what to do."

Silence settled between them. A minute, maybe more.

"I didn't leave because of you, Dylan." His name on her lips constricted the skin along his scalp. Her voice had barely registered over the soft pulse of his heartbeat behind his ears, and a rush of heat flared up his neck. "Not completely."

What the hell did that mean? "Explain."

"It doesn't matter that the New Castle Killer was found dead this morning. Not to me." She studied the curve of the beer in her hand a little too thoroughly, almost as though she was determined to look anywhere but at him. "I'm relieved his victims and their families will finally have the closure they need if we can prove Del Howe was the killer, but that case will haunt me for the rest of my life. Not because of the way they died but because I was humiliated when the people recalled me as sheriff.

"I've dedicated every moment of my life after I realized I was the only survivor of the fire that killed my family to saving anyone I could. But I couldn't save those men. I couldn't even get them justice. Someone else did, and the shame—the guilt—of letting them down was too much to handle. I had to start over. I had to move on. I had to forget that case, forget the people I worked with." She raised her attention to him. "I had to forget the man I was sleeping with, so I could simply move on with my life."

Thickness swelled in his throat as her words took shape one by one. "Is this your way of telling me you're not that into me, or that you think what we were doing was to blame for a killer getting away with murdering three victims?"

"Whoever killed Del Howe knew who he really was. They followed him here from Delaware then proceeded to murder him slowly and with great precision. Del Howe died with over eight dozen lacerations across his entire body, including his eyelids. Something like that takes time. It takes a lot of patience and a dedicated amount of research and planning." Remi stretched her hands across the table and leveled her chin. "Makes me think the killer we're looking for might've been in that house—same as you—to study their target, and if they were, they would've seen the surveillance photos of me in that closet. They would've known Del Howe was watching me."

Dylan leaned forward in his chair, the edge of the table cutting into his elbows. He tightened his grip around his beer bottle. "What does that have to do with anything?"

"The killer was obviously punishing Del Howe for what he'd done to his victims. Giving him a taste of his own medicine. Whether it's a family member or an officer who worked the original investigation, I can't say for sure, but that scene this morning said this isn't the work of a territorial serial. I think this killer's sole purpose might be revenge. It's personal for them. They're angry, obsessed and willing to kill. So they target the man responsible for making them feel that way, but in my experience, it doesn't stop there."

She traced an invisible pattern into the table's surface. "Hate is like that. It consumes and destroys until not even exacting revenge on the person to blame is enough. It builds until they can find a new target, the ones who are really to blame—the investigators who failed to bring their loved one justice in the first place, who let the killer get away. It doesn't matter who's to blame for the New Castle Killer slipping through our fingers or if I'm attracted to you or not, Dylan. We both made mistakes in that investigation, and there's a chance someone will try to make sure we pay for them."

Damn it. He'd known Del Howe had set his sights on her before the bastard had turned up dead, but the thought hadn't ever crossed his mind she could still be in danger. Whoever'd murdered Del Howe had already gotten what they wanted. Right? "What makes you so sure you're a target?"

"I wasn't the only subject of those photos, Dylan. Our entire team could've been surveilled, and anyone who worked that case might be at risk. Including you." Remi took a swig of her beer, those iridescent blue eyes darker than a few minutes ago. A soft ringing reached his ears from across the table, and she tipped to her right to pull her phone from her pants' pocket. Her theory made sense. If the killer had gone out of their way to track down and murder the person responsible for the three New Castle deaths, stood to reason the officers and investigators who'd failed to arrest the son of a bitch could be included on that list.

She swiped her thumb across the screen to answer the incoming call and hit the speaker button as Dylan pushed away from the table. "Watson, I wasn't expecting you to check in until tomorrow. Madison isn't going to do me any more favors from the district attorney's office if she thinks I'm making you work late."

Dylan cleared his empty beer bottle and the rest of his sandwich from the table and tossed them both into a freestanding garbage bag hanging on the pantry doorknob.

"She and the baby are asleep upstairs," Jonah said. Exhaustion weighed the deputy's every word. "This couldn't wait. I tracked down the investigating officers from the files you gave me from the New Castle Killer case. Two detectives working the case, four responding officers who arrived on each scene after Dispatch received the 9-1-1 calls, two crime scene techs—anyone who ever stepped foot onto those scenes."

Dylan faced the table, waiting, but he couldn't ignore the pool of dread solidifying at the base of his spine.

"Sounds like mostly everyone. I'm impressed you were able to track them down so quickly. I would've figured some of them had moved on from New Castle, maybe even crossed state lines or joined other agencies." Remi focused on the phone's screen, the creases deepening between her eyebrows.

The strong, assertive sheriff he'd been drawn to in Delaware had taken the wheel and shut down any evidence of their previous conversation, and his gut clenched. She'd drawn the lines between them. After everything they'd been through back east, after what'd happened in that cabin this morning, she'd made it perfectly clear nothing would get in the way of her finding this killer. Not even him.

"Have any of their credit cards showed activity in Oregon, or was there any evidence they'd been hunting the New Castle Killer on their own?"

"No," Watson said. "There's no evidence to support the idea any of the people who worked that case knew who Del Howe really was, and they certainly didn't follow him to Oregon."

"How can you be sure?" Remi cocked her head to one side but didn't lift her gaze from the phone.

A heavy sigh cut through Watson's side of the line. "Because they're all dead."

Chapter Four

Dead. Every single one of them.

Remi had ended the call with Jonah Watson more than twenty minutes ago, but she still couldn't wrap her head around the information he'd shared. The investigators from the New Castle Sheriff's Department had moved on with their lives after the case that'd destroyed her career had gone cold. They'd been promoted, taken on bigger cases and switched law enforcement agencies, but it hadn't been enough to keep them safe.

A fire in Nashville, a car accident in Kansas, a suicide in Wisconsin. She stared at the collection of newspaper articles Jonah Watson had sent to her phone. All of them. Gone. Every single investigator connected to the New Castle Killer case had been murdered, including the dispatchers who'd taken the 9-1-1 calls from family members and roommates who'd discovered the bloody crime scenes. Some were made to look like accidents, some like suicide, some like murder. None had been connected. Until now.

So many innocent lives.

"Remi." Dylan's callused hands slid into her peripheral vision as he reached for her from across the table. Dark hair laid flat against his muscular forearms, thick veins fighting to break through the underside of his arm. Rough skin caught on the back of her hand as he curled his fingers around hers, but his effort to anchor her into the moment failed. "It wasn't your fault. Not any of them. You couldn't have known."

"I need the case files for every one of these murders. The killer could've left something behind to compare to the evidence scene from the cabin." Remi shook her head, not entirely sure how to put the pieces together. She'd been trained in homicide investigations, but this seemed almost like a dream. A nightmare. "This is the work of a serial killer. He targeted each of them and methodically planned and executed their murders one by one. All because we weren't able to find the New Castle Killer."

"I'll pull the files from the federal database while you clean up. You've been running on fumes since this morning. You're no good to anyone like this. Take a shower, get some sleep and we can start fresh in the morning." Dylan released his hand from hers and left behind a warmth she hadn't realized she'd missed. "We're going to catch this guy, Sheriff. He's going to pay for what he's done. I give you my word."

He was right. She hadn't slept in over twenty-four hours since Gresham PD had called her to the scene at the cabin, and the longer she put it off, the less chance she had of not making a mistake on this case. She knew that, but her defense tactics had already been triggered when he'd brought up their previous relationship, and she wasn't about to show him any kind of vulnerability. Remi shoved to her feet, and the world tilted slightly to one side. "I'm fine."

Someone had killed all her friends, her coworkers, people she'd trusted and worked beside for years. Someone had hunted them down, was hunting her down. Hunting Dylan down. Her stomach rolled with the last realization. As much as she'd claimed she'd put what'd happened between them behind her, it was impossible to forget how she'd broken through his perfectly honed self-control. How he'd done the same for her. How, when they'd been together, neither of them had had to wear the mask they put on for the rest of the world or to keep up their guard. She'd missed that. Missed him. A flash of an image, of him meeting Del Howe's fate, shot across her mind, and her knees gave out.

Dylan rushed in to catch her before she collapsed, his chest pressed against hers. Strong arms encircled her as he settled her back into her chair, the spicy hint of his aftershave filling her lungs. "You never were a great liar. You have a tell."

"No, I don't." She couldn't think, couldn't breathe. She clutched his arm, ordering her legs to support her, but it was no use. The cracks in her armor had already started to spread. If she didn't get control of herself, she feared she might break right here in the middle of the damn safe house.

"You bite the inside of your mouth when you're lying." That voice, smooth and low, softened the resentment she used to emotionally defend herself against him. Him holding her reminded her too much of what she'd worked to leave behind, and she wasn't going to give in. Not again. "My guess is you learned to beat a polygraph by forcing your heartbeat to speed up with pain on the control questions, and you never kicked the habit."

"You can't possibly know that." Could he?

"I've seen it done enough in my former life as a private investigator, Sheriff, and I know you better than anyone else. I've seen who you really are." Dylan lowered his mouth to her ear, and a shiver ran down her spine. "You can't lie to me."

"I'm not a sheriff." Not anymore.

He helped her regain her balance on her own two feet, his hand still pressed into her lower back. Bands of heat swirled through her and she forced herself to step out of his reach. To prove she could. She wasn't a sheriff anymore, and he wasn't a private investigator anymore, but that didn't make the desire bubbling under her skin any less appropriate. She was the chief deputy of this district, his superior. If the United States marshal himself got even a hint of intimacy between her and Dylan, she'd lose her job and he'd be suspended.

She couldn't let the past ruin what she'd built here. For either of them.

Remi bit the inside of her mouth with her back molars to keep herself in the moment. He'd been right before. She had disciplined herself to pass the polygraph while in training at Glynco, and she couldn't seem to give up the habit when everything seemed so out of her control. The pain was the only way to get some of that control back, to remember there were still some things she could do to protect herself.

Someone was killing off anyone remotely tied to the New Castle Killer investigation, and she intended to find out why. She pressed her hand against her forehead, and the dizziness subsided. For how long, she had no idea. Didn't matter. She wasn't going to be able to sleep now anyway. "We need to pinpoint the locations where our suspect has killed and build a timeline of when the murders began. I want to see if there is a pattern we can discern from the data."

"We should also create an exhaustive list of anyone who was connected to the New Castle Killer case," Dylan said. "If we can find out where the killer is going next, we might be able to stop them."

Or who might be next.

"Watson is sending the files now. I'll get my laptop, and we can start there." Remi discarded her sandwich bag and half-drunk beer into the garbage sack and rounded back into the main living space. Hands on her hips, she took her first full breath since the moment Dylan had stepped through the door and let it out slowly. Her heart rate ticked slower at the base of her throat. There were too many similarities, too many connections between the New Castle Killer case and Del Howe's murder this morning. There couldn't be any mistakes this time.

Remi tugged her laptop from her overnight bag and headed back into the living room, her boots echoing off the open two-story ceilings. The laptop's aluminum frame cooled her warm skin as she closed the space between her and Dylan. Hypnotic gray eyes lifted to hers, and her heart stuttered in her chest. Three years. Three years she'd been able to hide from the New Castle case, from him, but the past had fully caught up with her. She settled in the seat she'd vacated minutes before and logged in to her email. The files were already in her inbox. Air caught in her throat as she counted the number of attachments. "There are twenty-five cases here."

Twenty-five victims.

Not even the most renowned serial killer in Chicago—The Carver—had officially claimed that many lives. The last time she'd checked with Deputy Finnick Reed and his witness, they'd attributed twenty to Jeff Burnes and his obsession to destroy women at the top of their fields.

Dylan leveraged his hands against the back of her chair and the edge of the table in front of her, and her awareness shot straight back into dangerous territory. "Who was the first?"

She scrolled through the attachments labeled with a case-specific identification number, and double-clicked on the last attachment, presumably the first link in this chain of revenge. The scanned documents filled her screen. The moment she recognized the victim's name, her gasp broke through the silence between them. "Teresa Hild was killed at her home in Greenville." Remi licked her lips as she read the initial incident report. "She was one of the uniformed officers who responded to the 9-1-1 call for the scene at Tony Rasmussen's apartment, the first victim we connected with the New Castle Killer."

"Scroll to the witness statements," Dylan said.

She used her middle and ring finger to slide up on the track pad, and the initial report slipped to the top of the screen. The witness statements were farther down in the file, past forensics, the superior case review and supplemental check-in reports. Dread pooled at the base of her spine. The New Castle Sheriff's Department had taken point on the investigation, and from what she could see of the highly organized file, they'd done a damn fine job. But the case was still considered open. No suspects had been noted in the file. "Neighbors reported nothing out of the usual the night of her death, and there weren't any signs of a break-in. Her dog walker found her the morning after. She let herself in with a key Officer Hild had given her."

"Maybe our killer did, too." Dylan eased back, taking the body heat he'd generated against her shoulder with him. "They question the dog walker?"

Right. Because men didn't have a monopoly on murder. "Her alibi checked out. New Castle Sheriff's Department doesn't have any real leads. The case has been sitting cold for nearly two years."

"What's the date she was killed?" he asked.

Remi shifted back to the initial incident report and leaned back in her chair. "Exactly one year after Tony Rasmussen's body was discovered."

DYLAN DIDN'T BELIEVE in coincidence.

Someone had used the date of the New Castle Killer's first victim's disappearance as a message.

Only that message had gone undiscovered for two years. The killer was intricately and deliberately hunting down everyone involved in the New Castle Killer cases. Every single investigator, but neither Dylan nor Remi had come across anything in the files that would lead them to a suspect.

"Next victim is Detective Diane Wiggs, killed in Maryland after she transferred to Baltimore PD a few months after I left." Remi took notes on the legal pad to her right then turned back to the laptop. Dim lighting darkened the shadows under her cheeks and eyes. They'd been at this for hours, but she wouldn't stop. She wouldn't let him see how exhausted she really was. Always out to prove she was the strongest, the most determined, the best. It was one of the qualities that made her a hell of a chief deputy. She wouldn't be distracted from an assignment, and she expected the same of her deputies, but sooner or later, the clock would hit zero.

Dylan marked the oversize map of the United States he'd found folded in the safe house's massive collection of books in the living room. Baltimore, Maryland. Check. They'd gone through half of the twenty-five files Deputy Watson had forwarded for their review, but no discernible pattern had showed itself. Hell, maybe there was no pattern, and the homicides weren't connected, but subconsciously, he understood exactly what they'd uncovered. A long string of murders to satisfy a deep-rooted desire for revenge, but from that initial spark, a serial had been born. Just as Remi had theorized. "Got it."

Who, of their current suspect pool, had the meticulous determination to hunt down and slaughter every single officer tied to the original case?

Jonah Watson had discarded the notion an original investigator had taken the law into their own hands. So far, the marshal had been right. They were all dead. A family member then? A partner they'd never known about ordered to finish what the New Castle Killer started? Hard to believe all these deaths were the work of one killer, but it was possible. The planning and locating of targets alone would take months, if not years. He wrote the date of the detective's death beside her push-pin on the map he'd taped to the wall and stepped back. "I can't make out a pattern here, Sheriff. This guy is all over the place. As far as I can tell he'd locate a victim then head straight there to add another notch to his murder post."

Remi set her chin into her palm and studied the map as he faced her. "You might be right, or he purposefully switched up which targets to hit and when in order to confuse law enforcement. If he'd killed his victims from the east coast to west coast, there was a chance someone would notice. Maybe the randomness is the pattern, same as the MOs he used to kill his victims. He didn't want any of them connecting back to him. No pattern, no way to determine his next step."

"Except we made the connection when we looked into the case." He folded his arms across his chest and pressed the edge of the pushpin into his finger. They'd narrowed down everyone who'd worked the investigation three years ago and compared the names to the files, but were there more? A dispatcher, a witness, an EMT they hadn't thought of?

"You made the connection." She pushed to her feet, and a yawn contorted her features as she headed into the kitchen for another cup of black coffee. "I ran as fast as I could as far as I could to leave this case behind."

Dylan rolled his lips between his teeth and bit down. "How is the killer getting the names of his targets?"

"What do you mean?" Remi refilled her mug and pulled one from the shelves, presumably for him. No end in sight for her—not tonight—but it was only a matter of time before the long hours caught up with her and she'd pass out wherever she landed. He'd watched it happen too many times before. Hell, the only reason she'd been able to give Gresham PD an alibi had been because cameras had caught her asleep at her desk around the time Del Howe had been murdered.

"I mean we didn't know some of these victims

were connected until Watson pulled their files and sent them to you, and we were working the damn case. Our theory is that the killer is murdering anyone involved in the New Castle investigation, but how did the killer know who was involved in the first place?" He crossed to the table as tendrils of adrenaline released into his veins. This was why he'd become a private investigator. This was what he'd been trained for. To take the smallest amount of evidence and suspicion and connect the dots.

He scrolled back through the open cases on Remi's laptop. Straightening, he pointed to the screen. "A family member wouldn't have been told the name of the dispatcher who'd taken the first 9-1-1 call or the name of the EMT who'd first arrived on scene. Those names are included in the initial incident report written by the officers on scene, and then detectives question them and submit their statements after the interviews."

The small lines between her eyebrows were back as Remi moved along the length of the kitchen island toward him. Her eyes widened. "You're right. Family members aren't briefed on who arrived on the scene, who collected evidence from the crime scene, who ran the samples in the forensics lab, yet every single one of them has been killed. So how is the killer getting this information, and how does he know their whereabouts?"

"I can think of one way." Occam's razor. The

simplest answer was usually the right answer, and Dylan didn't see any other way around it. "He's got to be law enforcement."

"We've already concluded it couldn't be one of the officers who worked the original case. According to Watson, they've all been accounted for, apart from you and me." Remi shook her head. She rounded the table, one arm crossed over her chest as she bit down on her thumbnail and bent at the waist to scroll through the files on her screen again.

His gut clenched. Watson's research had been thorough. The former FBI bomb technician was trained to spot the most minute details and uncover a suspect's motive, means and opportunity. Dylan trusted the marshal had tracked down anyone involved in the New Castle Killer case, including him and Remi. That meant the killer wasn't finished. If whoever killed Del Howe this morning truly had access to the files from the initial investigation, sooner or later the bastard would come for Remi, come for him.

And hell, having that information didn't only put the killer ahead of them, it strengthened Gresham PD's case against Remi. Only a law enforcement officer would've been able to access those files. The fact Del Howe had been following her, combined with the history between her and the

New Castle Killer case, would give them enough probable cause to seek a warrant from a judge.

But Dylan wasn't going to let her take the fall. This was what he'd been trained for, what all those years of off-the-books investigations had sculpted him into. No matter how hard Captain Elijah Paulson and his sergeant pushed to make her a suspect, Dylan knew without a doubt Remi hadn't done this. "We need to go through the background checks you originally ran for the first three victims' family members again. It's possible we missed something, maybe a law enforcement connection that didn't seem relevant at the time."

"I remember something like that coming back when we initially notified the next of kin for one of the victims. A distant relative maybe, but I can't..." Her eyes slipped closed—almost involuntarily—but she cleared her throat and set her expression. "I can remember. Just give me a minute."

Dylan trailed his hand up her spine and pried her away from the screen. She'd made it clear she'd rather forget what'd happened between them all those years ago, but he couldn't. He never wanted to forget. Never wanted to pretend it hadn't happened. For the first time in years, he'd found someone he could trust, who was as authentic on the inside as they claimed to be on the outside. He'd spent most of his life being lied to in one form or another, but with Remi, he'd never had to wonder if the words coming from that flawless mouth of hers were the truth, and it'd cleansed him in a way. Given him clarity. Helped him realize the culmination of keen observation skills and a lifetime of working on his own didn't have to hold him back. When she'd hired him, she'd made him part of a team, and he wanted more of that. He wanted her.

"You really can't handle your coffee. Come on, Sheriff. You know how embarrassed you get when you fall asleep on your keyboard."

Her voice softened as her words slurred together in an indistinguishable one-sided conversation.

Hell, she was about to collapse. Dylan maneuvered her down a hallway branching off from the kitchen, where the bedrooms had been laid out. Shouldering most of her weight, he passed the first door—a large bathroom—and headed for the second on his right. She wasn't going to make it to the end of the hallway. He kicked the door into the stopper behind it and flipped on the light.

A bare queen-size mattress had been centered in the room. Remi had told him the house had been acquired by the marshals service within the last two weeks. The case was still in the courts, which explained the lack of bedding, but it'd have to do. He swung her from his side to his front and braced his legs on either side of hers to keep himself from dropping her. Setting her on the mattress, he leveraged both hands against his knees.

She was still wearing her shoulder holster and her weapon. Damn it. He was going to have to figure out how to get her out of it without pissing her off. Or maybe sleeping with the thing was common practice for her nowadays. He had no idea. They hadn't shared a bed in three years. "Okay, Sheriff. I'm going to get you out of your holster. No biting, no kicking, no punching."

She mumbled something as her eyes slipped closed, and he couldn't help but smile. The woman didn't drink alcohol, but she certainly passed out cold as hard as any addict.

Dylan intertwined his fingers in hers and moved to thread her elbow back through the shoulder strap.

A strong grip shot up and locked around his wrist, those piercing blue eyes suddenly wide and aware. Remi wrenched her upper body off the mattress and dug her nails into his skin. "He's connected. Sergeant Nguyen...is...connected."

Her grip relaxed from his wrist, and she fell back, instantly unconscious.

Chapter Five

Sharp architectural angles came into focus as Remi cracked open her eyes.

Grogginess and the unrelenting ache of passing out when her body had given up weighed her down, something she'd become more used to over the years. Sleep hadn't been the same since she'd left Delaware. In sleep, the nightmares waited, and she battled every waking hour to push it off more and more. Until she couldn't. It was the perfect solution. Passing out ensured utter numbness. She'd burned the midnight oil a few too many times while she'd been sheriff back east. In those moments, she'd realized when her body simply gave out, there hadn't been any nightmares. No shame. No humiliation for what she hadn't been able to change. Over the past three years, that darkness had developed into a safe space, an emptiness she couldn't wait to hide inside. Sometimes it'd take a day, sometimes two, for the blackness to find her.

This time had been on the shorter side, and her stay even shorter.

She turned her head to one side, her hair catching on the divots in the bare mattress's structure, and the grogginess drained. Except the past had caught up with her. She bolted upright and instantly patted at her side. Her shoulder holster and weapon were gone…with her boots. Studying the room, she recognized the color of the bare wood trim around the closet, and brief memories of the night before surfaced. Watson had sent everything he'd had on the murders of her former coworkers and investigators involved in the New Castle Killer case. And Cove… She and Dylan had gone through them…together.

Remi wiped sleep from her eyes before attempting to roll off the mattress with some kind of grace. Instead, she rolled straight onto her shoulder holster, her weapon and her boots neatly waiting for her beside the makeshift bed. Her overnight bag packed with a few changes of clothes, toiletries, extra ammunition and a first-aid kit had been brought into the room, too. She stared at the strap coiling over the edge of the bag, feeling as though she'd made an important connection with the case, with who might've had something to do with Del Howe's murder, but she couldn't remember. One of the downsides of pushing herself into exhaustion instead of listening to her body when it needed to rest—damaged short-term memory.

She reached for her bag, unpacked a change of clothes and collected her holster and weapon from the floor. Slowly, she opened the bedroom door. Movement registered from down the hall, and she caught a glimpse of brown hair, bare muscular shoulders and a mountain of rock-solid deputy marshal. Dylan. He'd followed her to the safe house last night, brought her dinner, worked through the files Watson had uncovered.

Her mouth dried as he dropped to his hands and feet and counted off a series of pushups. Muscles she'd never known existed rippled across his back in a hypnotizing dance of strength, and she found she couldn't look away. He'd changed over the past few years. His dry sense of humor hadn't, but physically, he'd become rougher around the edges, less approachable to anyone who didn't know him well, more aggressive and…bigger. Tempting.

"Didn't anyone teach you it's not polite to stare?" Dylan hopped to his feet and turned to face her, sweat glistening down his chest and abdominals. Shadows carved defined ridges across his midsection as he reached for a nearby towel. A smile broke out across his handsome face as he wiped droplets from his hairline, and her gut twisted. From the smile she hadn't been able to forget or the fact she'd been caught watching him, she didn't know.

Remi tightened the grip on her holster to counter the heat flaring up her neck and into her face. "I figured it was fair game considering you removed my boots and holster after I passed out last night."

His laugh intensified the heat simmering under her skin. He brushed the hair hanging over his forehead back and collected his discarded T-shirt from the floor. He'd changed into sweats while she was asleep, leaving no doubt he'd stayed the night. "To be fair, you weren't unconscious yet. You were still talking, and I told you exactly what I was doing."

"Did I..." She cleared her throat while trying to sound casual. There'd been times—nights—when she'd screamed herself awake. Times she'd rather not reveal to a man who used to share her bed. "Did I say anything?"

"You said a lot of things. At one point, you recited the alphabet backward, and while I was unlacing your boots, you said you were going to kick me in my perfect face." Dylan tossed the towel then threaded both arms into the sleeves and stretched the T-shirt over his head. "Then you accused Sergeant Nguyen of having a connection to the New Castle Killer investigation."

"Sergeant—" The fog lifted, and a soft gasp escaped her control. "The background checks we ran during the initial investigation. I remember that same spelling coming up when we were trying to contact next of kin on one of the victims." She closed her eyes, trying to sort through the hundreds of facts she'd archived at the back of her mind, to those first few days of the case. "Tony Rasmussen. He was half Vietnamese. Most of his mother's side of the family had adopted Americanized last names when immigrated to the states, which made them harder to track down during the initial stages of the investigation, but there were a few who'd kept tradition. Sergeant Nguyen was one of Tony's uncles."

Could he be the killer? Had he discovered the identity of the man responsible for his nephew's death and killed him? Had he used his access as a Gresham PD officer to hunt and take his revenge on anyone involved in the case then used that same power to accuse her of Del Howe's murder? Was the sergeant she'd come to know these past few years the reason this was happening?

"I ran a background check on Daniel Nguyen while you were asleep." Dylan pointed to the kitchen table, out of sight, and headed that direction.

The corner of the hallway blocked her sightline of him, and Remi used those few seconds of isolation to take a deep breath. She hadn't allowed herself to feel much of anything after relocating to Oregon, but in those short moments Dylan had been unaware of her presence, she'd remembered what it'd been like to feel those muscles under her touch. Remembered how...safe she'd felt the times they were together, and a piece of her had craved that sensation again. Wouldn't happen. Not now. Never again. Not only because she was his superior, and a relationship with a subordinate would reflect poorly on her career, but because he was the link to a past better left forgotten.

Remi forced one foot in front of the other until she rounded the corner, and their makeshift murder board came into sight. Surprise filtered through the drugging haze of sleep as she took in the progress he'd made in the few short hours she'd been asleep. A complete set of pins had been set in the map that indicated the locations of each murder with dates written clearly in black marker. The butt of her weapon brushed against her calf as she closed the distance between her and the map. Distinct blue lines connected the locations, a trail of where the killer had been and where he'd gone next, dating all the way back to the first murder and ending with Del Howe's death in Gresham yesterday. "You did all this while I was asleep?"

"You were right about the randomness being a pattern in and of itself. Six of the twenty-five original investigators in the case were still in New Castle County when the murders started two years ago." The sound of his heavy footsteps filled her ears as he stepped up beside her, his arm brushing against hers. Dylan motioned to the entirety of the board. "He might've started there, but I think the killer was trying to keep law enforcement from catching on to him too quickly. He couldn't kill all six of them around the same time. Too much attention. So he spread it out. He killed Teresa Hild at her home in Greenville, then he headed to Georgia for the next." Dylan used his hand to indicate the blue line from Delaware to Georgia, the veins accentuated in the back of his hand. "Sometimes he'd alternate between New Castle County and his next location. Sometimes he killed two or three victims before returning, which makes me believe—"

"Delaware is his home base." Even now, there was a chance whoever'd killed Del Howe had fled the state, but her instincts said the game of cat and mouse wasn't finished. There were still two investigators here in Oregon who'd been involved in the original case. Her and Dylan.

Remi visually traced the patterns he'd created across the board, noting a red line had been added sometime during the process. A line that interconnected a few of the murder locations and dates, and ended in what looked like Gresham, Oregon. "And this red line? What's that one for?"

"After you suggested Sergeant Nguyen was involved with these twenty-five deaths—twenty-six, if you count Del Howe from yesterday morning—I started looking into him a bit more. We theorized our killer might be law enforcement, which would explain how he was able to get his hands on the original New Castle Killer case files. I think you were right." His chest pressed against her arm as he indicated the length of the red line, and warm, nervous energy skittered down her spine. Her breath caught as he continued. "I was able to verify Sergeant Daniel Nguyen was in these six cities when these murders occurred."

That couldn't be a coincidence. She'd been completely out of it when she'd claimed Daniel Nguyen was linked with the murders, but something at the back of her mind had made the connection. Now it was more than a theory. "Harrisonburg, Las Vegas, Hanover, Kansas City, Baltimore and San Antonio. All of these cities host law enforcement conferences. He could have used them as a cover to travel to these locations then slipped away long enough to kill his victims."

Dylan spun to her open laptop and angled the screen toward her. Six lists of names in distinct columns filled the screen, with one name highlighted on each page. Six pages, six lines, each matching the same name. Daniel Nguyen. "I reached out to the conference organizers after I made the same connection and had them send over their registration lists. It looks like that's exactly what he did. We can place him in these six cities at the times of these six murders. We also can't discount the fact he was the first officer who responded to Del Howe's murder scene yesterday morning. That still leaves nineteen murders we can't tie him to, but what are the odds this isn't our guy?"

"We'll need more than a registration list to prove he actually attended the conferences. Travel records, receipts, hotel reservations." Remi traced her finger across the trackpad of her laptop and focused on Nguyen's Gresham PD photo. "But it's enough to have Captain Paulson bring him in for questioning."

FLORESCENT TUBES ABOVE reflected off the yellowing tiles around the interrogation room. Dylan folded his arms across his chest as he leaned against the wall near the one-way glass. The scents of sweat, body odor and bodily fluids he'd rather not think about from the hundreds of suspects previously questioned in the room filled his lungs.

Sergeant Daniel Nguyen was the latest.

"What the hell is this, Captain? You said you had a few questions for me about yesterday's scene. Why are we meeting in here?" Daniel Nguyen's brown gaze cut from his captain to Remi in the seat across the table from him. "And what is she doing here? She was banned from stepping anywhere near this investigation."

An animalistic growl vibrated up Dylan's throat. His arms lowered to his sides as battle-ready tension hardened the muscles across his shoulders. "*She* is a federal chief deputy United States marshal, and you'll talk to her like one, Sergeant."

Remi's chin angled over her right shoulder, putting Dylan in her peripheral vision, but she didn't respond. She didn't need him to defend her, he knew that, but he wasn't going to stand there and let Nguyen talk down to her, either.

"We're just talking, Daniel. That's it. The conference room is being set up for the union meeting taking place in an hour. No need to read into anything." Captain Elijah Paulson tapped the file folder in front of him, the one Remi and Dylan had handed over to him less than an hour ago with the alleged connections between the sergeant and the twenty-six murders. A long trail of white-gray facial hair shook as the captain spoke.

He'd flat-out denied his sergeant had had anything to do with the New Castle Killer case and the resulting murders of everyone involved, but in the end, with the evidence Dylan and Remi had gathered, the captain couldn't ignore the truth. "Marshals Barton and Cove brought some information to my attention today, and I wanted to sit you down and clear the air. For all of our sakes."

Nguyen's expression flattened as he interlaced his fingers across the steel surface of the table. He leaned back in his chair, seemingly at ease, confident. "Then ask."

"The medical examiner identified the victim found at the scene as Del Howe." Remi slid an older photo of the man they believed to be the New Castle Killer across the table toward the sergeant. "Have you heard that name before or seen the victim prior to responding to the 9-1-1 call yesterday morning?"

Nguyen placed his hand over the photo and brought it in for a closer look. In less time than it'd taken him to blink, he pushed it back toward Remi. "No."

"Are you familiar with the New Castle Killer case?" she asked.

Visible tension bled into the sergeant's neck and arms. He shook his head but refused to meet anyone's gaze as he tried to force a casualness into his body. "No."

"Daniel." The captain kept his voice far more gentle than Dylan would have in his position. "According to your birth records, you're related to one of the New Castle Killer's victims. Tony Rasmussen. You're his uncle, his mother's brother."

Sergeant Nguyen closed his eyes, pressing his mouth into a tight line. His callused fingers arced over the table between him and his interrogators, the whites of his knuckles proof he was straining to keep up the façade. He stroked one hand down his face as he realized he'd been caught in a lie. "What happened to Tony doesn't have anything to do with the Howe investigation."

"We believe Del Howe was the New Castle Killer. We believe he was the one who killed your nephew." Dylan watched for the faintest hint of surprise or of being caught off guard, but Sergeant Nguyen kept his control in place. Interesting. "But you already knew that, didn't you?"

Nguyen's head shot up, panic creasing the lines around the edges of his eyes. "What are you talking about? I didn't kill anyone. I bring murderers to justice, not take the law into my own hands because she couldn't find the man who butchered my nephew." The sergeant motioned to Remi, and an explosion of anger spread behind Dylan's sternum.

He peeled away from the wall. "You have no idea how far she went to recover your nephew, Sergeant—"

"You admit you know who Del Howe really was then?" Remi said. "That he was the man who killed your nephew."

"I knew." Defeat took the fight out of the sergeant's expression, and he collapsed into the back of his chair, hands below the table where Dylan couldn't see them. "Do you know what that son of a bitch did to my family? He didn't just kill my nephew. My sister hasn't said a word since she received the news her only kid won't be coming home. She couldn't handle it. Her husband couldn't, either. He left her. He didn't know how to deal with her grief, and my sister had to be institutionalized. She stopped taking care of herself, stopped eating. Her body is alive, but my sister died that day your detectives told her Tony was dead."

"Is that why you killed Del Howe?" Dylan straightened. "The sheriff's department didn't get to him fast enough, so you took matters into your own hands? Did you think killing the bastard responsible for taking away her son would help her recover?"

Nguyen set his hands back onto the table and picked at the cuticles at the base of his nails. "That was my plan."

"Damn it, Daniel, what the hell did you get yourself into?" Captain Paulson scrubbed a hand down his face.

"I didn't kill him." The sergeant's square jaw worked overtime as he leaned forward over the table. "Believe me, I wanted to. I had the detectives assigned to Tony's case update me on any new information, but once they stopped responding to my requests, I couldn't sit there and watch my sister waste away. I had to do something. I called in every favor I had to get copies of the files on all three victims and dove into the case myself. The first few months, I had nothing. There were no new leads, the killer seemed to have gone dormant, you were fired from the sheriff's department and the police had all but given up on finding Tony's killer."

"How did you uncover the killer's identity?" Remi asked.

The sergeant's mouth flattened into a thin line. "I paid the New Castle County medical examiner for the toxicology report after the second victim's—Brett Smith—autopsy. From there, I was able to trace the sedative found in the remains to a website selling it on the black market. I threatened the administrator, and he gave me the credit card information of all the buyers who purchased the drug three months before the Tony went missing."

"Del Howe was on that list?" Dylan asked. "Where is the report now?"

"I destroyed it." Daniel Nguyen's head dropped as the reality of that decision hit him. Setting one hand on the edge of the table, he enunciated every other word with a tap of his fingers. "I didn't want anything leading back to me after I'd finished with what I wanted to do to him. Only, I never got the chance. Someone beat me to it yesterday morning. You have to believe me—I didn't kill him."

"So your alibi for the murder is that you couldn't have killed Del Howe because you were in the middle of planning how to kill Del Howe." That was a new one. Only problem was, with the destruction of a key piece of evidence, Daniel Nguyen couldn't prove he hadn't had anything to do with Del Howe's death.

"There's already evidence leading back to you, Sergeant. Every officer involved in your nephew's case has been systematically hunted down and killed over the past two years." Remi took the file folder from Captain Paulson and opened it flat onto the table. She skimmed through the first few pages inside then slipped one sheet across the table.

It was a printout of the registration information Dylan had collected from the conference organizers early this morning. "We have proof you registered for law enforcement conferences in these cities within these dates I've written along the tops of each list from the organizers." She handed him another piece of paper from the same file. "During which six investigators were murdered in those same locations. How would you like to explain that?"

"I... I can't." Confusion rippled the lines stretched across the sergeant's forehead as he studied the documents in front of him. "I wasn't in these cities on these dates. Wherever you got this registration information from, that wasn't me."

"A credit card in your name was used to register for each conference, Daniel." Captain Paulson's voice deepened with a combination of disappointment and sorrow. It was his turn to pass a collection of documents to his officer. "I had the cyber crime squad run your financials after Marshals Barton and Cove brought this to my attention. We can match the payment information to a card opened two years ago when the killings first started."

"But did you check these dates against my shift schedule?" Nguyen asked.

"We have one of our marshals double-checking the dates and interviewing your partner now. But, Sergeant," Dylan said, "you're going to want to get ahead of this while you still can. Del Howe was dead approximately eight to twelve hours before the 9-1-1 call was logged. You haven't given us an alibi that proves you weren't at that cabin before you responded, and you've been linked to at least six of the twenty-six murders we've uncovered during this investigation. Chief Deputy Barton can put in a good word with the district attorney, but you're going to have to give us something here. Something that shows us you're telling the truth."

"I had nothing to do with any of this, and my shift schedule will prove it. I didn't register for those conferences because I've wasn't at those conferences." Daniel Nguyen pressed his index finger into the table. "I was here, doing my job.

If they were paid for with a credit card in my name, check with the credit reporters. My house was broken into two years ago while I was on graveyard shift. All that was taken was the binder where I keep my personal documents. It was in my fire safe. Birth certificate, social security card, passport—anything someone would need to steal my identity."

A flood of hesitation washed through Dylan as the sergeant shook his head. "Whoever you're looking for, it's not me. But you'll be hearing from my lawyer and my union rep all the same." Nguyen turned his attention to Remi. "You were the one Del Howe was surveilling, Chief. I wasn't the only law enforcement officer with a grudge against him."

Chapter Six

Remi closed the door to the interrogation room behind her, the evidence file against Sergeant Nguyen in hand, and faced Dylan and Captain Paulson. "I don't know about you, but I don't read him as a killer. There are too many pieces to this investigation. They all seem to fit, but I think he's telling the truth."

"It'll be easy enough to check when the credit card used to register for the conferences was applied for and activated, and to look into the break-in he claims happened two years ago." Dylan folded his arms across his chest, accentuating powerful muscle fighting to break free from his T-shirt. He nodded toward Captain Paulson. "You can check in with the officer we asked to run the dates of the murders against Nguyen's shift schedule. Should give us some answers as to where we go from here."

Remi ignored the warmth bubbling behind her

sternum. Dylan had stood up for her in that room when Nguyen had pointedly blamed her for what'd happened to his nephew. Unnecessary, but it was the thought that counted. The US Marshals Service had been born and bred as a boys' club since the seventies, and it'd taken every last ounce of her fight to land her position as chief deputy. Nobody had helped her along the way. Nobody had supported her. That was the way she preferred to rise through the ranks, by her own merit, but that didn't minimize the appreciation she had for him right then.

The captain shook his head. "As much as I hate the idea one of my own is involved with what happened to Del Howe out in those woods, I gotta admit, I don't feel bad for the man if what you said is true."

"Believe me, nobody does, but that doesn't mean his killer should go free. No one is above the law." Remi exhaled hard as she came down from the last few adrenaline-fueled minutes. "What do you think our chances are of getting a search warrant for the sergeant's house? He claims he destroyed the toxicology report that led him to Del Howe, but maybe there's still something we can use to prove he wasn't the one who killed the vic."

"I'll call the judge now to let her know what we have. If she's in a good mood, your chances are high." The sound of Captain Paulson's heavy footsteps bounced off the tile floor as he headed for his office.

Daniel Nguyen's last words echoed in her mind. He was right. The sergeant wasn't the only law enforcement officer who held a grudge against Del Howe, and the evidence inside the victim's closet had proved it. The New Castle Killer had been closing in on her, putting the entirety of her team at risk. She would've done anything to keep that from happening, to keep them safe, including the deputy at her side.

"I can read your mind, you know." Dylan's voice pulled her attention back into the moment. "The sergeant might not be the only officer who wanted Howe to pay for what he'd done, but the evidence against him is a hell of a lot stronger than what they have against you. They can't pin the New Castle Killer's death on you, Sheriff."

There was that word again, the label she'd taken so much pride in when she'd served New Castle County.

Remi slid her hand into her cargo pants as the tattoos on her forearm itched for attention, but that was an itch she'd never be able to scratch. Not as long as she kept running from the past.

"I doubt Daniel Nguyen killed any of those victims, including Del Howe. His shift schedule won't match up with the conference dates and the credit card company will reveal his identity was stolen. I'm sure of it. Whoever killed the New Castle Killer used his identity in order to frame the sergeant and to get access to the department's personnel files. The killer learned he was the uncle of one of the victims and made him the perfect fall guy." Remi started toward the captain's office.

A strong grip surrounded her arm and twisted her into a wall of muscle. Dylan's exhales swept across the overly sensitive skin of her neck as he lowered his voice, and her nerve endings caught fire. "Everyone involved in the case has been targeted and killed. I'm not going to wait for him to catch up to you."

His body heat penetrated her long-sleeved shirt and warmed her insides, and Remi fought the urge to lean into him more, to revel in the connection between her and another human being. Not just any human being. Dylan.

She'd left Delaware behind for a reason, but her heart had yet to catch up with her logic. She'd run from the past, but a piece of her held fast to what they'd had together. However casual she'd written them off then, the same couldn't be said for now. She lowered her voice, sure to keep their conversation between them. "You know as well as I do, anything we find in that house won't be admissible in court if we don't wait for a search warrant."

"If we have Daniel Nguyen's permission to search, we don't have to wait," he said.

Confusion flooded through her. “Then why have Paulson call the judge for a search warrant?”

“Because I want the captain focused on clearing his sergeant’s name instead of on the fact you could still be a suspect.” Dylan’s grip loosened, but he didn’t release her completely. Steel-gray eyes lifted above her head, distant. He was trying to protect her. But, truth be told, he was more at risk of becoming a suspect in Del Howe’s murder than she was. The surveillance photos proved the New Castle Killer had been closing in, but the forensics was sure to prove Dylan had been in that cabin before the body had been discovered by Annabell Ross and her hiking partner.

Remi shifted her stance to keep the captain in her peripheral vision. “The killer is either law enforcement or is using Sergeant Nguyen’s identity to access law enforcement files. Once the captain confirms his officer was working during the dates and times the victims were killed, the suspicion will be back on me. The more evidence Gresham PD uncovers, the less we’ll be able to convince them I’m not involved.”

“I’d guess we’ve got about thirty minutes before he realizes where we’ve gone,” he said. “Should be enough time to get a head start.”

“Okay.” She had to think through this and ensure the consequences of investigating on their own didn’t blow up in their faces. “You get written permission from the sergeant for us to search his property. I'll get the gear." Setting her hand over his heart, she pressed her fingertips deeper into the hardened muscle. His pulse beat strong beneath her palm. "Be careful."

Dylan set his hand over hers and squeezed. "I'll meet you in the parking lot in five."

She handed him the file and headed for the bullpen of officers, ringing phones, witnesses and offenders. Nervous energy skittered down her spine as the captain's door swung open, but she'd already reached the glass double doors leading to the parking lot.

Pushing outside, Remi sucked down a lungful of fresh air and headed for her SUV.

Shadows surrounded the single parking lot light illuminating her vehicle. Unnatural light from the station's doors reflected off shards of glass as she closed in, and a knot of warning twisted in her gut. She studied her SUV and slowed her pace. Something wasn't right. She adjusted the weight of her weapon a split second before she turned back toward the doors leading into the station.

A fist slammed into her face.

Lightning shot across her vision, and the world slipped out from under her.

Remi shoved off the pavement with both feet to use his own weight against her attacker. They hit the asphalt together. Oxygen crushed from her lungs, but she couldn't wait for him to make the next move. Catching her breath, Remi spun him toward her and launched her fist into the perpetrator's face. She knocked him off balance as he tried to stand. Wrapping both hands around his wrists, she threw him into the light pole and drew her weapon. "On your knees, hands behind your head. Now!"

A low, even laugh penetrated through the sound of her pulse pounding in her ears. "Did you really think you could run from me, Sheriff Barton? That you wouldn't have to pay for your failure like the rest of them?"

Her heart shot into her throat as she reached for the cuffs at her lower back.

"You killed them. Everyone connected to the New Castle Killer case. Why?" Nausea churned in her gut, hot and heavy at the same time. Forgetting the cuffs, she slipped her finger alongside the trigger of her weapon. "Who are you?"

"I'm the one who made sure Del Howe couldn't take another innocent life." The suspect straightened against her orders, standing at well over six feet. He rushed her, and Remi squeezed the trigger. The bullet grazed his neck but didn't slow him down. He shoved his shoulder into her midsection, hauling her off her feet and slamming her into the side of her SUV. Her weapon fell from her hand and slid under the vehicle, out of sight.

She couldn't breathe, couldn't think, as he pressed his hand into her throat, pinning her against the warm metal. Dark eyes glared at her through the holes in his black ski mask. He lowered his voice, nearly pressing his mouth to her ear. She tried to push him back. "I've waited a long time for this, Sheriff. I killed the others, but none of their deaths had been personal. Just their punishment for following your orders. Your death—what I'm going to do to you… I'm going to enjoy the memories for the rest of my life."

"Remi!" Dylan's voice carried across the parking lot. Her gaze cut to him. The deputy withdrew his weapon, danger in his gray eyes, but didn't fire. There was no guarantee he'd hit his target. "Let her go. Now."

"Don't worry, Cove. I haven't forgotten about you." Her attacker pulled his own weapon and fired.

"No!" Remi lunged for the gun, but it was too late.

Dylan clutched his side and collapsed to his knees.

Her scream cut off under the pressure of her assailant's grip around her throat. The parking lot—Dylan—blurred in her vision as that same hand rocketed her head into the driver's-side window and the world went black.

HE TOOK HER. The son of a bitch took her.

Dylan compressed a hand over the wound as a

swarm of officers surrounded him on either side. Gravel bit into his palm as he forced himself to his feet. He stumbled forward as blood spread across his shirt. He closed his eyes and tried to catalog everything he'd seen. "Male, six-four or six-five, wearing a ski mask, black clothing. I didn't see what type of gun he was carrying, but the slug in my gut will tell you that." Pain vaulted through his system and threatened to bring him back to his knees, but this time a set of callused hands held him up.

Captain Elijah Paulson. "Somebody get this man an EMT, damn it, and pull the surveillance footage from that camera! What kind of vehicle, son? I'll dispatch two patrols now."

"He took her SUV." Dylan rattled off the license plate from memory. He holstered his weapon and pulled his phone from his pocket with bloody, shaking fingers then pulled up the app Remi had required all her marshals to install in case of emergency. One step forward. Two. He caught sight of some kind of wiring where the chief's vehicle had been parked. "Every marshal's vehicle is equipped with GPS. He knew that." Dylan nodded toward the collection of wires. "He was waiting for her."

But the killer wouldn't kill her outside a police station. He'd take her somewhere else. Somewhere no one would be able to find her. Dylan struggled across the parking lot, his steps growing heavier as he headed for his own SUV.

"Marshal Cove, where are you going? Wait for the EMT. All units, be on the lookout for a black SUV heading north on Eastern. Vehicle is registered to Chief Deputy Remington Barton." Captain Paulson's voice phased in and out between his ragged breaths. "Marshal Cove!"

He wasn't going to wait for the EMT. He wasn't going to sit here while Gresham PD figured out who to send after her or where to look. From what he'd been able to tell from the files Watson had collected on the twenty-five victims tied to the New Castle Killer case, Remi didn't have that kind of time. The killer didn't keep victims for extended periods of time. He killed them as soon as he saw the opportunity and moved on to the next. A growl vibrated up his throat and aggravated the bullet in his side. "No."

He couldn't lose her—not again—but he wasn't going chase after a killer without knowing exactly what he was getting himself into either. He had to think. Dylan ripped open the driver's-side door of his SUV and collapsed inside. A groan tore from his chest as the muscle shifted around the bullet. Phone in hand, he direct-dialed Finnick Reed. When the marshal's witness had been taken by a serial killer, Reed had been able to narrow down her location by studying the habits of the man who'd taken her. If anyone knew how to get Dylan to Remi, it would be the former combat medic.

"Reed," the marshal answered.

"The chief has been abducted by Del Howe's killer." Dylan twisted his keys in the ignition and spun out of the parking lot as Captain Paulson and his officers raced after him. He floored the accelerator and steered the vehicle with one hand while he tried to apply pressure to his wound with the other. "She's injured. I'm not sure how bad, but I need you to tell me where the bastard might have taken her."

"Wouldn't hurt you to ask nicely for once." The echo of keyboard taps filtered through the phone.

"Reed." Another growl tore from Dylan's chest as his anxiety over finding Remi in time increased. Frustration formed as he searched traffic patterns for an SUV going extremely faster than the speed limit. The killer had taken a high-ranking marshal. That meant he'd want to get the hell away from the scene as fast as he could, but Dylan couldn't pick out any vehicle matching Remi's description. The suspect had already veered off in another direction in an attempt to keep from being followed.

"Calm down. I've been studying your guy's movements since our little meeting back at the office. He doesn't stay in more than one city very long before moving on to his next victim. This doesn't seem personal to him. It reads more like a job than anything, but according to Remi's notes, there wasn't only one victim here in Portland the killer was targeting. There were three," Reed said. "Del Howe, Remi and you. I don't think this guy is going anywhere until he's finished what he started. He'll have to be somewhere close to the city in order to get access to his victims, but not close enough he won't be able to hightail it out if the police catch up to him. Somewhere where there'd be no neighbors to hear a scream."

"You're saying he's not in the city. He's just outside of it." The on-ramp to the interstate that would take him west out of Gresham then north when it connected to the 205, out of the city—that would be the fastest way to escape. His instincts said Reed was right. The previous victims might've been a job as Reed had suggested, but whoever'd taken Remi had been building to this for years. Blamed her. He wouldn't kill her quickly. He'd make her suffer. He was sure of it. That the killer needed privacy and time to exact his revenge on the investigators involved in the case, but that left a lot of options in the way of location.

Dylan maneuvered ahead of a group of vehicles and accelerated onto Interstate 84. He searched every lane ahead of him for the familiar SUV. The killer only had a few minutes of a head start, but Dylan knew from experience a few minutes was more than enough to seal Remi's fate. "I need more, Reed."

"According to CCS, Remi's phone just pinged from a tower near Burton Ridge in Vancouver, north of the city," Reed said. "But it hasn't moved in a few minutes."

Across the Columbia River. The killer had gotten farther than Dylan had originally thought. Determination burned through him. She wasn't dead yet. He had to believe that. He had to believe the killer would take his time with her and give Dylan a chance to make it. "Send me the coordinates."

"Camille and I will dive back into the files Watson recovered and narrow down a location where he might've taken her. Keep me updated." Reed ended the call.

His phone pinged mere seconds after the line went dead. The small red dot on his screen assigned to Remi's phone wasn't moving, and he pushed the SUV harder. The dull sound of tires against cement droned in his ears as he sped across the bridge into Washington State. She wasn't going to die. He wasn't going to make another mistake.

Maneuvering between eighteen-wheelers and civilian vehicles, he spotted the exit leading to Burton Ridge and crossed three lanes of traffic to take it. His heart lodged high in his throat as miles of rolling black mountains and shadowed trees materialized through the windshield. If the killer had taken Remi into the wilderness, it'd take days for Gresham PD and USMS to search the woods.

He was catching up to her signal. Soon, he'd be directly on top of it. Dylan tightened his grip on the steering wheel as his eyes adjusted to the darkness along the off-ramp. His headlights illuminated the stop sign at the bottom of the decline. Bright lights from a convenience store right off the interstate honed his focus as the signal identifying his phone rolled over Remi's.

Dylan slammed on the brakes. The bullet in his side jerked deeper into muscle with the added momentum and pried a muted scream from his chest. No sign of another vehicle. No sign of a body. Darkness closed in around the edges of his vision as he put the SUV into Park. He called in his position to the Gresham PD officers he'd lost in the chase. His weapon sat heavy in his holster. Shouldering out of the vehicle, he stepped out into nothing but fine dirt and shadows. Headlights illuminated a narrow path straight ahead of him but failed to alleviate the dread pooling at the base of his spine as he searched the tree line.

The killer had crossed state lines. He could've gone anywhere with Remi by now, but something inside—some part of him that'd been connected to her these past few years—said Dylan was on the right path. Dirt kicked up in front of his headlights as he rounded the front of the SUV. The GPS on her phone placed her right here, but suddenly, the red dot indicating her phone's signal was moving. She was here. Hand resting on the butt of his weapon, Dylan approached the trees. He hadn't come all this way to lose her. They hadn't survived this game only to be separated again. That wasn't how this would end.

Movement shifted in the trees to his left, and every sense he owned honed on the break in the leaves. "Deputy US Marshal Dylan Cove. I need you to come out, slowly, with your hands where I can see them. Now."

A soft whimper reached his ears then another shift of the branches ahead. "I'm sorry!" a frightened voice said. A woman appeared from the surrounding shadows and stepped into the peripheral of his headlights. Dirty red hair dulled in the light, her clothing stained and torn in places. "I wasn't trying to steal it. It was lying there on the road, and I didn't think anyone would miss it. You can have it. I won't tell anyone. I promise. Please." Wide eyes lowered to Dylan's weapon as the woman stretched her hand forward and offered him a phone. Remi's phone. "Please, don't hurt my son."

Dylan loosened his grip on his firearm as a pair of small hands appeared from behind the woman's leg. He holstered his sidearm and presented both of his palms straight out toward the woman and her kid. "It's okay. I didn't mean to scare you. I'm a US marshal. I'm not here to hurt you. That phone you have? It belongs to another marshal who was abducted about thirty minutes ago. I tracked it here. Can you tell me where you found it?"

"Over there at the edge of the road." The woman used her chin to indicate where she'd picked it up. She slid her hand down her son's back to press him closer. One wrong move on his part and she and her son would disappear, and Dylan didn't have the time to chase after her. The clock was already counting down for Remi. "He threw it out the window before he sped off."

"Did you see if he was wearing gloves?" If he could pull a print from the phone, Reed would be able to narrow down the perp's identity. Dylan took a step forward, keeping his hands raised as he approached the duo. "Did he say anything, or did you happen to see the marshal he'd kidnapped? Do you know where I can find her?"

Fear contorted her features and the woman hugged her kid tighter. Staring down at the ground, she seemed to disappear into a memory right in front of him before lifting that hesitant gaze to his. The woman shook her head. "You're too late. She's already dead."

Chapter Seven

Her head pounded in rhythm to the chaotic rush of blood behind her ears.

Dust caked the inside of her mouth as she struggled to open her eyes. Smooth rocks pressed against her abdomen and chest as she rolled her head to rest her opposite cheek against the hot ground. Sharp pain rocketed through her skull, a dried, crusted layer of something wet and sticky clinging to one side of her face. Blood. Pitch black surrounded her, the ground uneven and sloping. Thick humidity clung to the skin of her face and neck. She heard her own rapid heartbeat—fast and flighty—along with the whisper of her breath. Heard everything except what she wanted to hear the most: Dylan. He'd been shot trying to stop her abductor from taking her. Where was he now? Had he been found? Was he alive?

An agonizing ache set up residence in her shoulder sockets as she tried to bring her hands forward, but her kidnapper had bound her wrists behind her back and her ankles together. Coarse, fraying edges brushed against her fingers. Rope. Whoever'd hunted down and targeted her former officers and investigators had caught up with her, but she wouldn't go down without a fight. Not with Dylan's life in the balance.

"These lava tubes extend for miles underneath the earth, all throughout Oregon and Washington. You'd be amazed how easy it is to get lost if you don't know what you're doing." The faint voice rolled along the corridor, bombarding her from every direction to the point Remi wasn't sure where her abductor stood.

An onslaught of blinding light filled the chamber and forced her to look away from the figure standing directly over her. She hadn't heard him approach. Hadn't even heard him breathe. "I've spent months mapping as many of them as I could, but there doesn't seem to be an end." He paused. "Well, not for you, Sheriff."

Caves. Lava tubes. He'd brought her underground. She tried to swallow past the dirt caked around the inside of her mouth as her vision adjusted to the new source of light. The headlamp blacked out his features, leaving only a silhouette of the man above her. She didn't recognize his voice, his outline. Nothing at all that would give her an ID. But the fact he'd attacked her outside the Gresham police station while Nguyen was still in custody said the sergeant had been telling the truth all along.

Remi squinted up toward the light, her shadow casting a dark pool around her. Then the pain surfaced. The dirt had been stained with blood. He'd pulled off the freeway, taken the exit and maneuvered to the side of the road. It'd been an opportunity to run, but when she'd climbed over the back seat into the cargo area, he'd been there. Waiting. The flash of metal was all she'd seen before the blade had embedded into her side. Now she was on the verge of going into shock, bleeding out, somewhere no one would be able to find her. Remi spit the dust from her mouth. "It's chief deputy marshal now, but you already knew that, didn't you? You've been looking for me, trying to find the perfect opportunity to get to me. A year, right? That's how long it's been since the last murder."

"Would've been sooner if you weren't so much of a workaholic. I couldn't exactly kill you in your office with the rest of your team in the building, and when you weren't falling asleep on your keyboard, you seemed to take added security precautions. Always armed, sleeping less and less these days, pushing yourself harder with each assignment, and then there was the added problem of Deputy Cove following you like a good little guard dog." Her abductor's knees popped as he crouched beside her, his voice even and unemotional. "It's almost as though you knew this day would come, that you knew you couldn't hide from your mistakes forever."

A rock settled in her stomach as she realized how thorough the man balancing her life in his hands had been. Both he and Del Howe had been following her all this time? Remi settled her left temple against the ground. What were the chances? "The surveillance photos. You were using Del Howe to watch me. You knew who he was, what he'd done, and you used it for your own agenda. When he served his purpose, you killed him in the same manner he'd killed his victims."

"What's a little blackmail between killers?" A laugh penetrated the buzzing in her ears. "Besides, you know what they say about payback. But look on the bright side, at least now the families will know who killed their sons, brothers and nephews. Thanks to me, the victims of the New Castle Killer finally get the closure they deserve."

Remi closed her eyes against the piercing pain at the back of her head and tried to focus on the rope binding her wrists. If she could loosen it enough, she'd be able to escape. She could run. Pressing her left side into the ground, she realized her abductor hadn't only taken her weapon, he'd removed her holster completely. She opened one eye to face the blinding light spilling over her as she pried one thumb underneath the binding around her opposite wrist. "Right. Because I'm sure that's why you've killed twenty-six people—to give the victims' families closure. Not out of a sick sense of revenge for him hurting someone you loved. Who was it then? Whose name do you use to convince yourself you're doing the right thing by executing the team who devoted their lives to bringing him justice?"

A fist slammed down directly in front of her face. Her abductor's hand trembled with the tension running through it as blood spread across his knuckles. Thin raised lines crisscrossed the back of his hand, scars, but he pulled back as quickly as he'd struck. "Was taking the private investigator you hired to find Tony Rasmussen, Brett Smith and Tad Marrow to your bed part of that devotion, Sheriff? Is that what you call it? From what I can tell, you were far more invested in your own selfish pleasure than bringing Del Howe's victims home."

A short laugh burst past her lips.

"You think you know me, but I did my job. I did everything I could to find those victims and stop him, and I lost everything because of it. We all did. You're not going to convince me I could've done more. None of the people you've murdered these past two years could've done more." Remi pulled her head off the ground and faced off with her assailant. A man who'd killed innocent people for his own perverted cause.

"You might not call this little crusade of yours revenge, but you've blinded yourself to the truth. No one could've saved those victims. Not even you." The rope around her right wrist slackened, and she set her head back against the ground to get a better angle from her shoulder. "You're no savior. You're nothing but a cold-blooded killer, just like Del Howe."

One second. Two.

"I think I would've liked you in a different life, Sheriff. We're alike, you and me. More than you'd imagine. Only, I'm the one who's facing the truth now." The light ascended closer to the ceiling of the cave as her abductor stood then disappeared altogether.

Darkness settled over her in a unforgiving, relentless cloak of uncertainty. No sign of him, except the faint echo of his breathing. "You were right about one thing, though. I am a killer, and tonight, you're going to know exactly what it's like to be a victim."

Remi heard his quick approach and rolled as fast as she could toward the wall illuminated by his headlamp earlier. Loose rock and wide breaks in the ground cut into her arms as she wrenched away from his attack. She couldn't see, could barely hear over the pounding of her heart, but her survival instincts would get her through the next minute, the next hour. She had to believe she'd make it out alive. Her shoulder hit the wall and she pressed her back into it to make herself as small of a target as possible. She tugged at her ankles, but the rope wouldn't give. She'd have to free her hands if she had any chance of getting the hell out of here.

"This is my favorite part. The hunt. The fear, the rash decisions you'll make in order to give yourself the slightest chance of survival. I made a lot of your colleagues' deaths look like accidents, but we both know how this is going to end, Sheriff." Her attacker's headlamp came to life, and she ducked her head to avoid the assault on her senses. "You can't hide from me. Even if you manage to run, you'll be lost in these tubes for days. No food. No water. No calling for help. No chance of saving your deputy."

Dylan.

"You shot Deputy Cove in the process of abducting me. If you've done as much homework on him as you have on me, how long do you think you'll last before he catches up to you?" Because if there was one thing she could count on, it was Dylan's need to make things right. For the victims of the New Castle Killer case. For the teammates he'd let down. For her.

She pressed the backs of her hands into the wall of rock behind her and gasped at the sharp slice of pain near her wrist. Blood trickled across the sensitive skin. Would the shard be sharp enough to cut through the rope? Even then, how fast could she counter an attack with her feet still bound?

Remi maneuvered the small section of rope between her wrists against the rock and jerked her hands down, but the rock fell away. Despair slithered through her as her abductor approached, and she pressed her heels into the ground to sit straight against the wall.

"I think the more relevant question, Chief Barton—" he reached out, fisted a handful of her hair and forced her to stare straight up into the light from his headlamp "—is how long do you think you'll last down here with me?"

"WHAT DO YOU mean I'm too late?" Dylan didn't dare approach the woman or her son. They were the only leads he had to finding Remi. He couldn't risk spooking them and them taking off with the information he needed to get to his chief. "What did you see?"

"Your friend, the marshal you're looking for, she tried to escape, and he stabbed her." Tremors racked the woman's hands and up her arms. "She wasn't moving when he forced her back into the SUV." She shook her head and hugged her son closer. "I'm sorry. I can't help you. He can't know I was here."

"She..." Remi had been stabbed. No. He shook his head in an attempt to come up with another explanation, something that didn't involve a murderer once again taking the only person he cared about. No, no, no, no. That wasn't part of the plan. The killer wouldn't have gone to all that trouble of abducting her from the Gresham PD parking lot if he'd planned to finish what he'd started in Delaware so quickly. He was supposed to take his time with her. He was supposed to give Dylan a chance.

His ears rang as he tried to make sense of the events the woman described. He lowered his hands to his sides. Remi had changed the plan by trying to escape. She'd fought back, forced her abductor to make a rash decision and paid the price.

"Which direction?" His voice sounded hollow, unfamiliar even in his own ears.

"What?" The fear was back in the woman's expression, the uncertainty.

"Where did they go?" he asked.

She pointed to the freeway, and a rock settled in the pit of his stomach. The son of a bitch had only pulled off the interstate to get rid of Remi's phone. He could've taken her anywhere by now. Dylan reached into his back pocket and extracted a handful of bills from his wallet. He had no idea how much, but he wasn't going to take the chance the killer would come back to look for witnesses. He offered the money to the woman and her son.

"Here's enough to get yourselves a full meal and a room for the next couple of nights. Leave the phone. And whatever you do, don't come back here."

The woman snatched the cash from his hand and backed away slowly, as though he'd attack, then tossed the phone right at him. Without another word, she latched onto her son and ran for the trees, taking the last account of Remi being alive with her.

Dylan stared down at the phone, dread pooling at the base of his spine. The GPS would be useless, but the phone itself might have something of use. Gravel and dirt crunched under his boots as he rounded to the rear of his SUV and hefted the hatch above his head. Every marshal under Remi's jurisdiction was required to carry emergency supplies and a forensic kit.

This was an emergency.

He tugged a tackle box from the back of the space and flipped it open. After snapping a pair of latex gloves into place, he extracted an evidence bag and collected the phone from the dirt. US marshals were in the business of protecting witnesses, transporting high-profile criminals and fugitive recovery, not forensics. But that wasn't going to stop him from doing anything he could to save the sheriff who'd given him a new purpose in this damn world. The woman who'd found the phone had most likely smeared or destroyed any fingerprints that might've been left from the killer, but Dylan couldn't risk leaving the device behind.

His phone vibrated in his pocket as he secured the evidence in the lockbox at the back of his vehicle. Peeling the gloves from his hands, he answered the incoming call. "Tell me you have something."

Because from the description the witness had given him, Remi was already out of time.

"CSU's report from the scene at Del Howe's cabin was issued a little less than an hour ago. They found a small section of tire impressions that matched the treads of a marshals service SUV. Looks like someone had tried to destroy evidence they were ever there." Tension raced down Dylan's spine at Reed's next words. "And my gut is telling me you might know who."

Not someone. Him. Damn it. He'd missed a section of mud when he'd been there three days ago. He'd entered the cabin legally with the help of the property's owners, but any other evidence the forensics team uncovered of him being there, combined with his past experience on the New Castle Killer case, only strengthened Gresham PD's theory Remi was involved. Dylan cleared his throat. "They were mine."

"Well that makes my life easier. I take it you weren't there on marshal business or you would've told us sooner." The distinctive sound of rustling paper filtered through the line. "In addition to that section of treads, Forensics found a complete set of footprints coming from the tree line and stopping directly under the window at the south side of the cabin. Scratches indicate a crowbar had been used to unlock the window from the outside. Can I credit you with that, too?"

"I had a key from the cabin's owners. I didn't need to use a window." The south window. That didn't make sense. "That was where the hikers said they were when they discovered Del Howe's body inside, but that doesn't explain why they would try to break into the cabin."

"Or why there was only one set of footprints instead of two," Reed said. "The prints are from a pair of well-known size twelve hiking boots. According to the hikers' statements, they were together when they discovered Del Howe's body yesterday morning, but that doesn't look like that's the case."

Dylan's head pounded in rhythm to his racing heart. The hikers had lied when they'd given their statement to Gresham PD. "We need to talk to them again."

"Captain Paulson has already dispatched two patrol units to bring them in. Gresham PD collected the hikers' boots at the scene, but I asked him to put a rush on the lab work. So far, there hasn't been any answer at Annabell Ross's home, and they can't seem to get a permanent address for her hiking partner, Henry Sallow." A high-pitched squeak pierced through the phone. Reed's chair. "The footprints leading up to the window had traces of volcanic rock in the treads, which stood out, considering the last volcano to erupt around that area was Mount Saint Helens in '80. Hard to believe traces would have survived all that time unless they were fresh."

"Did you say volcanic rock?" Dylan narrowed his gaze on the ramp leading back onto the interstate, which would keep taking him north.

There'd been a story in the news the past few months about a group of central Oregon hikers who'd discovered miles of new lava tubes and caves longer than geologists had originally thought running straight from Mount St. Helens. Some of which had never risen to the surface. If the hikers who'd called 9-1-1 about Del Howe's body had been part of the small group of explorers, they could've had traces of the rock in their boots and would have an intimate knowledge of the caves. Was one of them Remi's attacker?

That was where her abductor had taken her. That was where he'd find Remi. Adrenaline dumped into Dylan's veins as he stumbled for the driver's seat and slammed the door behind him. The wound in his side screamed as he started the SUV and sped toward the on-ramp. He set the phone in the passenger-side seat on speaker. The article he'd read about the caves only specified the general area where the cavers had discovered the entrance to the tunnels. He needed more than that. "Get the United States Geological Survey on the phone. Tell them we have a marshal who's been abducted, and we need to know the exact coordinates near my location to the lava tube caves recently discovered."

"On it. I'll send you the map as soon as I have it." Reed ended the call.

Time stretched into a distorted fluid, seconds into minutes, minutes into what seemed like hours. Congested lanes and landscaped terrain bled into open road and miles of trees and towering mountains. So different from Delaware, the life he'd left behind to follow Remi into the marshals service, but Dylan didn't have attention for any of it. He couldn't lose her. Not after everything they'd already survived together.

While he'd initially crossed the country to find Del Howe and make up for the mistake of not listening to the killer's last victim, Remi had been the one who'd gotten him to want to stay. The DOJ had believed a former private investigator diversified the array of men and women who'd taken up the federal shield, but many chief deputies around the country didn't trust the way he'd built his reputation by being suspected of circumventing the law.

Didn't trust him. After his application had been accepted and he'd finished his four-month training in Glynco, Georgia, Remi had offered him a position in her district. She'd given him everything at the risk of losing her job. Given him a purpose. He wasn't going to turn his back on that.

The ping from his phone ripped him back into the moment. He couldn't right the mistake he'd made with the New Castle Killer case, couldn't help any of the bastard's victims or catch the killer himself, but he wouldn't fail Remi. His knuckles fought to break through the skin on the back of his hands as he strengthened his grip around the steering wheel.

Dylan swiped his shaking fingers across the phone's screen, and a map replaced his call history as he sped north. The US Geological Survey had forwarded an updated map of the lava tube entrances. The nearest opening was at least ten minutes from his current location, and he'd already pushed the SUV as hard as he dared. Ten minutes. Remi had been abducted, knocked unconscious with the help of her driver's-side window and stabbed, according to the woman who'd picked up the chief's phone.

She was running out of time.

Chapter Eight

"Do you know how much blood the human body can lose before it goes into shock?" her attacker asked. "I do."

A glint of metal blinded Remi right before stinging pain sped across her upper arm. A single strike. Nothing compared to the stab wound in her side, but her heart couldn't tell the difference. Her pulse hiked, and her fight-or-flight instincts revved up a notch. Only, she couldn't run. The headlamp swept across her arm as blood trickled from the newest wound. She pulled against the ropes at her wrists and ankles with everything she had.

A low, menacing laugh filled the cave and echoed back to her. His outline above her grew larger as he closed the distance between them. "I cut Del Howe over one hundred times before he started to lose consciousness. Nausea, sweating, shallow breathing. He lost a lot of color as his toes and fingers went numb. You see, the body tries to compensate when blood pressure drops. Considering how much you've already lost, Sheriff, soon your heart will try to keep up with less volume."

Another quick slice of the knife across her midsection lit up her nerve endings, and she shuttered a groan at the back of her throat. "He begged me to stop, you know. Just as his victims had done over and over, but I have a feeling you're not like my other victims. You won't beg for your life, will you?"

"How…would you know Del Howe's…victims begged?" The scars across his hands. The faint raised lines she'd noted when he'd slammed his fist into the ground near her face. Remi set her head back against the smooth rock supporting her from behind, trying to fill her lungs. Her stomach churned as sweat beaded in her hairline. Her body had already started sliding into shock. She was losing too much blood. From her head, from the stab wound in her side, from the new lacerations across her skin. "You were one of them, weren't you? One of the New… Castle Killer's victims."

Pieces of the puzzle started falling into place. The timing of those first murders—a year after the last victim had been taken—the targeting of her colleagues and officers, the methodical patience and hatred it must've taken to torture and slowly kill Del Howe. Cut by cut, scream by scream. Remi closed her eyes against the hurling dizziness in her head. A victim would blame the investigators who'd failed to bring them home. "We never recovered…the last two bodies."

"No, you didn't." Footsteps, farther away now, reverberated off the walls around her, and she forced herself to stay conscious enough to track them with her eyes closed. Memorize them in case he switched off the light again. "Do you know how Del Howe got into my apartment building? He used his job as an elevator inspector. I'd noticed him on more than one occasion, which, now that I think about it, was unusual. How many inspections did a single elevator need, after all?"

The beam from the headlamp had been firmly turned away from her. Remi pulled her wrists apart and set her teeth as the coarse strands ripped sensitive skin in the process. Her lack of vision suddenly felt as though it were crushing the oxygen from her veins. She had to keep him talking. Distracted. "He was casing the…building. Looking for…a target."

"And he found one." Her attacker hadn't moved. "I came home, unlocked my door and went inside. Same as I did night after night. He was already waiting for me. He'd picked the lock on the dead bolt and hid in my coat closet. I hadn't realized I wasn't alone before he'd knocked me unconscious." A hollowness had entered her abductor's voice, still unmoving across the cavern. "When I woke up, I was tied to a chair with rope, duct tape over my mouth. I couldn't move. Couldn't even scream as he cut me over and over. I thought each slice of his blade would be my last, but the nightmare never ended. Not until I'd blacked out."

"You survived." Remi stilled as the rope around her wrists slackened with stretch. He couldn't see her. Not without turning the headlamp on her again, and she had enough strength left to take advantage. Arching her back, she pressed her elbows as close to one another as she could and shimmied her hands up and down until the rope slid down the length of her fingers. The pain in her side intensified, but she couldn't scream out. She brought her hands forward, relieved for the increased blood flow to her aching shoulders. Leaning forward, she stifled the groan building in her chest as agony tore through her midsection. Blood spread across her shirt and flowed into the waistband of her pants. Sticky. Warm. She couldn't think about that right now. Couldn't focus on more than getting the rope around her ankles loose. "How?"

"I still ask myself that same question. Somedays, I think it was basic survival. Adrenaline, faster reflexes, a basic instinct to live." His voice had grown louder, closer, and desperation clawed through Remi at the realization. The headlamp hadn't moved from its position about ten feet away, but her attacker had. He was closing in, using the darkness to his advantage. How? "Other days, I recognize what Del Howe brought out in me the day he stole my life."

"And what's that?" Silence descended all around her. Panic overtook her, and she rushed to get free of the rope at her ankles. Only the sound of her shallow breathing filled her ears. She pulled a strand loose, and the rest of the maze of rope around her ankles fell apart. Kicking the ties away, Remi stumbled to her feet, her back against the wall.

There wasn't enough light produced by the distant headlamp to give her any idea of where the exit was, but she could follow the wall long enough to get the hell away from her would-be killer. Her nails dug into the soft stone as she sidestepped along the perimeter of the cave. Run. Hide. Escape. There was no other option in her condition. Particles of dirt fell around her shoulders and head with every step, and she covered her nose and mouth with the crook of her inner arm. She couldn't afford to make a single sound. Not if she wanted to survive this.

"My own kind of monster." A fist connected with the side of her face.

Lightning streaked across her vision, and she hit the cave floor. Remi barely had time to wonder how he'd found her in the shadows when his boot struck her ribs. Pain, unlike anything she'd experienced before, overwhelmed her nervous system and tore a scream from her throat. The headlamp's dim light outlined her attacker enough for her to block the second strike to her midsection, and she latched onto his foot and twisted as hard as she could.

The hard drop of his body kicked up dust into her face and eyes. She couldn't see, couldn't think. Dirt and shadows had stolen her vision. She couldn't rely on the light if she was going to get out of here. Remi scrambled to her feet, her fingertips using the cave walls as guidance. She pumped her legs as fast as she could and held one hand above her head to stop herself from running into lower sections of ceiling. Her palms burned with friction, but she wouldn't stop. Couldn't.

"You're going the wrong way, Sheriff..." The taunting undertone in his voice echoed in her ears, but Remi only forced herself to keep going. "The faster you run from me, the faster you seal your own fate. You'll never get out. Not without me. Oh, and mind the drop."

Drop? The floor disappeared from beneath her feet, and her heart lurched into her throat. Her backside slammed against the angled cave floor. Rock and solid bubbles of cool stone tore holes through her pants and shirt as she fell countless seconds. Five? Ten? Her feet were the first to hit solid ground, and her legs collapsed out from under her. She rolled twice—three times—before settling flat on her back. A groan escaped her control as she clamped onto the stab wound in her side. The sob bubbling in her chest ached to break free, but she wouldn't give in to the hopelessness churning inside. Not yet. She might be running in the wrong direction, but the alternative meant running toward her abductor's knife.

Remi fanned her free arm out to one side and hit a rough formation sprouting from the ground like cairns of stones fused together. The floor here seemed to be constructed of the same bubble-like shapes as in the section of the cave her assailant had held her, reminding her these tunnels—these tubes—had once been molten lava. Cool air brushed against her overheated skin. She held her breath and waited for the sound of her kidnapper following her down the drop.

Only the fast-paced beat of her heart interrupted.

She couldn't stay here. Even without the added pressure of a killer on her trail, she needed food, water, medical attention. Dylan had been shot. As much as she was certain Gresham PD had gotten him the help he'd needed, she couldn't leave him with the uncertainty. She couldn't let him spend the rest of his life trying to find her as he'd spent the past two years hunting for the New Castle Killer. That wasn't the life he deserved.

He deserved more. A partner, a family, someone he could trust and rely on. Someone to ease the burden he'd carried all these years trying to right the mistake he'd made. He deserved to be happy.

Hell. She wanted to be the one to make him happy. The gut-wrenching realization punctured the protective layer she'd held on to since losing her family in that fire. But if the killer believed she'd died in theses tunnels, he'd go after Dylan next, and she'd never forgive herself. Emotions led to vulnerability. Vulnerability led to mistakes and losing the people she cared about, and she couldn't lose him.

Remi rolled onto her uninjured side and forced herself to sit up. Her head collided with a low section of cave ceiling, and she automatically brought her hand up to test the extent of the drop in height. It seemed to go on forever. She maneuvered onto her hands and knees and crawled forward. These past six months, Dylan had forced her to confront her failures and shame. No matter what happened, she wasn't going to run this time. Not from him.

TIRES SKIDDED ACROSS the dirt as Dylan slammed on the brakes in front of the cave entrance. The call for backup had gone out a few minutes before, but he wasn't going to wait. Remi didn't have that kind of time. He reached into the glove box for a flashlight. Exiting the SUV, he unholstered his weapon and rounded the front of the vehicle. Knee-high weeds rustled as he moved into position.

The sun had gone down hours ago. It would be a maze inside with or without the flashlight, but that wasn't going to stop him from getting to her.

Cool air brushed against the underside of his jaw as he pressed his back against one wall and craned his neck to search inside the entrance. No movement. Nothing to suggest an ambush. Yet. Barely more than four feet wide and five feet tall, the entrance to the cave seemed to breathe on its own. If the map hadn't told him exactly where the entrance had been located, he would've missed it completely, but his instincts and a fresh set of footprints in the dirt confirmed he was in the right location.

His harsh exhale echoed back to him as he heel-toed it along one wall. He clicked the flashlight to life, scanning the ground in front of him. Rough, bubble-like formations threatened to throw him off balance with each step. Cracks spread out from sections of rock, indicating the ground itself had settled over time.

What appeared to be yellowing stalactites clung to a large section of the ceiling to his left. He managed to avoid a dip in the ceiling height as the entrance tunneled in four separate directions. Dylan paused. Remi could be down any one of the tunnels. One wrong choice, one mistake, and he'd lose her forever. Not an option. Searching for the footprints he'd noted in the dirt at the entrance, he followed a path to the tunnel on the far left. "I'm coming, Sheriff. Hold on."

The hairs rose on the back of his neck as he ducked into the largest of the four tunnels. If Remi's abductor had had to carry her in here, Dylan imagined this was the tunnel he'd used, but there was still a chance these passageways were empty, and he was on a scavenger hunt that would end in his own death.

The cave floor declined under his boots, and thousands of tons of rock suspended above him bled into focus. Goose bumps prickled across his arms as temperatures dropped. Caves had their own climates. Species of animals and organisms never found anywhere else on the planet. Glancing back toward the entrance, he calculated he'd walked about one hundred feet. How far would the killer go to ensure Remi was never found?

A brush of something against his arm twisted him around. His stomach rocketed into his throat as the flashlight worked to reveal whatever'd run into him. Small squeaks reached his ears and echoed off the walls. Bats. He must've clipped one when he'd—

A wall of muscle slammed into him and anchored him against the opposite wall. His weapon fell from his grasp, lost in the darkness. Shards of rock dug into the muscles between his shoulder blades as he struggled to refill his lungs. Dylan gripped the flashlight, braced the underside of his fingers with the cylinder and shoved away from the wall.

His attacker ducked his shoulder into Dylan's midsection and spun to squeeze his arm around Dylan's neck.

Dylan hauled his fist into the bastard's kidney. Once. Twice. A groan filled his ears. The flashlight beam grazed his dropped weapon, and Dylan lunged to collect it. Pulled back by his clothing, he swung his elbow up and over and connected with the son of a bitch's face. The slack between him and his opponent disappeared as the suspect hauled Dylan straight back into his spine and flipped Dylan onto his stomach.

Pain exploded from one side of his rib cage and aggravated the bullet still ripping through the soft tissue in his side. Dirt caked his mouth as he struggled to take a full breath.

"You've come to take my prize from me," the outline above him said.

"What can I say? I'm a selfish bastard." Dylan

launched himself toward the gun, knocking it farther out of reach just as a heavy boot slammed into his lower back. Sweat built at the base of his neck and ran down beneath the collar of Dylan's shirt as he climbed to his feet. The beam from the flashlight barely illuminated the room let alone highlighted his attacker, but Dylan had been in enough situations to learn to trust his senses.

"Ah, but the sheriff is more than a colleague, isn't she, Cove? She's the reason you stopped being a private investigator and came to Oregon." Remi's abductor swung a hard left, but Dylan was faster.

Blocking the strike, Dylan gauged the suspect to be around six-four, at least two hundred and twenty pounds. A high-pitched ringing filled his ears as he relied on everything but his vision. He kicked out, connecting with the suspect's knee and forced his attacker to the ground. Dylan stood over him, battle-ready tension hardening the muscles down his spine. "Where is she? What did you do with her?"

A low, unsteady laugh bounced off the walls around them and solidified in the pit of his stomach. "You know, I'd tell you, but that would be cheating."

A hard fist rocketed into Dylan's temple and knocked him off balance. He slammed his forearm into the next hit, took a punch above the bullet hole in his gut and struck out. His knuckles met flesh and bone and knocked his attacker off balance. Momentum, exhaustion and blood loss took the strength out of his legs, and he hit the ground. Cold steel pressed into his shin under his weight. Dylan wrapped his hand around the gun and got to his feet. He brought his weapon up and took aim.

Only, the assailant had disappeared.

"Where are you?" His breathing ricocheted off the formation of stalagmites climbing from the floor toward the ceiling. Dylan crouched to collect the flashlight from the ground, every cell in his body on high alert for movement. Another tunnel took shape a few feet away.

"Do you think she knows, Cove?" a voice whispered from the shadows. "Has the good sheriff figured out the real reason you applied for the marshals?"

"You don't know what the hell you're talking about." Not possible. The killer's words gutted him deeper than the bullet still lodged in his side. Remi had spent her entire life guarding—protecting—herself from the people around her seeing the vulnerability she denied existed, but Dylan knew better. He recognized the effort she put into carrying her division with her strength, of being the woman the team could rely on. Knowing the real reason why Dylan had come to Oregon and not the reason he'd given her when he'd walked into her office six months ago would only break the trust she'd built with her deputies. With him.

Dylan followed the voice one step at a time. Blood seeped from his wound and down his pant leg, his footsteps uneven. "Run all you want. Del Howe couldn't hide from me, and neither can you."

"I'm not the one running out of time, Cove." Dirt cascaded from a nearby wall, and Dylan slowed. "You're bleeding out. Soon, your body is going to go into shock just as the sheriff's did after I stabbed her. So are you going to come after me with the last few minutes you both have left, or are you going to save the woman you're lying to?"

Remi. His ears rang. Dylan pulled up short. He couldn't leave her here to die. No matter how much he wanted to make up for the past, she needed him to get her the hell out of here. "I'll be seeing you later, you son of a bitch."

Taking the main tunnel around to the right, he pressed a hand over the bullet wound in his side and jogged as fast as he could. The toes of his boots dragged with every step, but blood loss, exhaustion and disorientation weren't going to stop him from finding her. "Remi!"

His voice reverberated off the sides of the cave.

No answer.

She was alive. Because no matter the reasons he'd had coming to Oregon, applying for the marshals service, he couldn't let her go. Not when they'd been together in Delaware, and not now. She wasn't just a means to an end or a way to relieve stress from an impossible case. She was everything. His rock, his anchor, his purpose. Without her, he'd have lost himself in a haze of rage and guilt a long time ago, and he couldn't become that person again. "Remi!"

Movement registered ahead, and Dylan slowed two steps before a wild swing of sharpened rock nearly sliced across his throat. He stumbled back, a throaty and desperate scream filling the cavern as she lunged at him. Dylan shot one hand out, catching her wrist midstrike, but he wasn't fast enough to catch her other hand.

Pain arched through his face as her fist connected with his jaw, and he dropped the flashlight. Landing on his back, he kept her at arm's length as she raised the rock over her head to strike a second time, pure survival contorting her features.

"Remi, it's me!" He ducked one foot under her shin and rolled her with every last ounce of strength he had, pinning her beneath him, her wrists to the floor. She bucked her hips to get free, and Dylan released his grip. "It's Cove."

"Cove?" Her voice softened. The diluted beam from the fallen flashlight highlighted the overwhelming tension between her shoulders and neck. Sobs visibly racked through her as her head fell back against the ground. "I'm sorry. I thought you were him. I thought—"

"I know. It's okay. You don't have a damn thing you need to be sorry for." He pulled her into him, holding on to her through sheer force of will as numbness swept through him, and set his mouth to the crown of her head. "I'm going to get you out of here."

Chapter Nine

White light and muffled voices overwhelmed her senses. Survival automatically urged her to open her eyes, but a safe sensation of numbness and warmth spread through her and dragged her deeper. Only this time, she didn't want to go deeper. Pure, comforting numbness was all that waited—no nightmares, no pain, no guilt—but where she'd retreated to that space over and over again in the past, it wasn't good enough anymore. Not after her abductor had nearly taken his revenge.

"Take it easy. Wouldn't want to have your nurses have to restrain you again." That voice. She knew that voice. Coaxing and dangerous at the same time, a perfect combination that promised to bring her back to the surface.

Remi clung to it, battling to bring herself past the drugging haze of unconsciousness. Piercing fluorescent light intensified the stiffness in her neck and shoulders, and flashes of the headlamp that'd kept her attacker's identity in shadow scored across her mind. She turned her face from the outline above her and tried to raise her hands to block the light. Stinging pain shot along her arm.

"You've got an IV in your arm, Sheriff. Try not to tug it too hard." Warm, callused fingers coaxed her arm back to her side, and it took everything inside her not to pull away at the physical touch. Steel-gray eyes came into focus before Dylan looked up at something across the bed. "Dim the lights for me, would you? They're bugging her eyes."

Movement shifted from somewhere within the room as the brightness eased. Coarse sheets, white tile, a door with a bright silver handle. A hospital room. Soft beeping filled her ears from one side of the bed. A loose blood pressure cuff encapsulated one arm, the catheter for her IV line in the other. Bubbles floating in clear liquid filled the thin plastic tube. Fluids. She must've been in worse shape than she'd originally estimated. "How long…?" Rawness coated the entire length of her throat, hints of dirt still clung to the inside of her mouth. Her voice had lowered an octave, unrecognizable even to her own ears. "Unconscious…?"

"You came out of surgery about four hours ago." Dylan smoothed a section of her hair away from her face, and a buzz fizzled across her over sensitized skin. That was the second time he'd touched her in as little as two minutes. "The surgeon was finally able to stop the internal bleeding and sew up your wound, but you lost a lot of blood between the caves and the hospital. You lost consciousness right after I got you into the SUV. Your doc wants to keep you overnight to make sure your vitals stay stable. Then there's the cut at the back of your head and the concussion you endured when your kidnapper took you from the station."

Her eyes were still heavy, but the fact Dylan was standing by her hospital bedside at all eased the last few hours from her memory. "He shot you. I thought...you...were dead."

"Nah. It's a flesh wound. One of the ER doctors pulled the slug. We've sent it to ballistics to match it to your abductor's weapon. With any luck, we'll be able to tie him to at least one of the murders Watson uncovered." A seriousness erased the smile from his mouth as he stared down at her, and her gut clenched at the rapid change. "I wasn't going to let a bullet stop me from getting to you, Sheriff. You're too important."

A lightness flooded through her as those last three words settled between them. Important to the team or important to him? Did it matter?

"Do you remember anything your kidnapper said? Maybe some identifying factors that can help us narrow the field of suspects?" Deputy Finnick

Reed pushed off the wall near the door and closed the distance between them. Inquisitive blue eyes—masking his usual sarcastic nature—settled on her. "There's a chance the hiker who called in about Del Howe's body is our guy, but it seems he gave Gresham PD a fake name and address. Turns out Annabell Ross, his hiking partner that day, barely knows him. Only met him a couple weeks prior to that hike in a caver group she's part of. He's not answering his phone. No one can find him."

Images of those thin white scars across the back of the suspect's hand shot to the front of her mind. She could do more than that. "He's a victim."

"What do you mean?" Dylan asked.

"One of the New Castle Killer…victims." She motioned to her opposite hand, the one limited by the IV line. "I saw the scars on his hand. He told me how… Del Howe targeted him using his job as an elevator inspector, how the killer had broken into his apartment and waited for him to come home. He was…knocked unconscious. When he woke up, he'd been tied to a chair by the wrists and ankles with rope and had duct tape over his mouth to keep the neighbors from hearing him scream."

Confusion contorted Dylan's face a split second before he hid behind that all too familiar controlled expression. "You're sure?"

She nodded.

"Well, hell. No wonder your man has targeted

every investigator involved in the case. He's out for revenge. Not for a family member, as we originally believed, but for himself." Reed crossed his arms over his chest, the superhero logo of today's T-shirt bright white in the shape of an elongated skull. Fitting, considering Reed had been the one to punish the Carver for the women he'd manipulated and killed, including the marshal's witness-turned-fiancée. "You didn't happen to catch his name or recognize him in the middle of that damn cave, I imagine?"

Images of pain—of desperation—demanded attention, but Remi wouldn't let them out. Wouldn't let her team see the cracks beginning to form. She diverted her attention to the cold sensation building in her toes. Whatever painkiller the surgeons had used to keep her sedated during surgery had started wearing off. She fisted her sheets, preparing for the pain. "No."

"Investigators were never able to recover the last two bodies in Delaware. All that was left at each scene was a life-ending amount of blood. It's possible one of Howe's victims escaped, and that would explain the string of murders we're connecting now. Although, how someone had survived all that..." The wheels visibly turned in his gaze as Dylan worked through the new information. He straightened. "That narrows the pool down to two possible suspects. Brett Smith and Tad Marrow."

She didn't miss the dip in his tone at the mention of the last victim, the one he'd failed to protect from the New Castle Killer, and her heart jerked in her chest. He still blamed himself for what'd happened to Tad Marrow, and despite her revelation that she wanted to be part of the solution—to be the one to help him move forward—she imagined he always would. "Unless there's a fourth victim we don't know about."

"You think that's a possibility?" Reed asked.

"At this point, we can't…discount anything. He's killed twenty-six people across the country. That takes a lot of time, a lot of planning and a lot of…patience." She raised her gaze to Dylan's, completely at ease as he studied her. He'd saved her life in those caves, even after she'd tried to attack him. That kind of debt couldn't go unpaid. "He failed to kill us once. He'll do whatever it takes to make sure he doesn't…fail again."

Reed uncrossed his arms as reality settled between the three of them. "You've got yourselves a unique kind of serial killer. He's not doing this out of compulsion. There's no MO connecting him to any of the murders he's committed. No pattern that can predict his movements. This is straight-up retribution. Both of you need to get the hell out of Dodge."

"Give us a minute, Reed. There's something the chief and I need to talk about." The weight of

Dylan's attention pressurized the air in her lungs. Hardness bled into his features, accentuating the muscle and veins under warm skin.

Remi felt raw. Exposed. Every inch of her insides ached. Her emotions had been stripped of the protective layer she'd built over the years. A killer had abducted, stabbed and nearly killed her. She'd almost died in those caves. Would have if it hadn't been for Dylan.

Reed closed the door behind him, leaving her alone with Dylan and feelings she'd denied for years. Feeling climbed up her legs, and she internally panicked for the return of sweet numbness. Because without it, she feared the current of feelings she'd held back all these years would suck her under the surface and tear her apart. "There's something you didn't feel comfortable enough saying in front of Reed?"

"You were kidnapped, stabbed and tortured less than six hours ago, Remi." The shock of her name on his lips tunneled beneath the heavy layer of emotional denial and straight into bone. His voice held nothing of the authoritative, aggressive deputy US marshal she'd hired six months ago, the one who'd sworn what they'd had together in Delaware wouldn't affect their working relationship as marshals. This was the Dylan Cove who'd worked past her defenses so easily during the New Castle Killer case, they might as well not have been there at all. He closed the space between him and the edge of her bed, sliding the tips of his fingers against her wrist. "I'm the only one here. You don't have to hide what you're feeling from me. You can trust me."

Tightness swelled in her throat, and she forced herself to focus on taking slow, even breaths to counter the effect. She bit the inside of her mouth to keep herself in the moment, to keep herself from constantly replaying the bone-shattering strikes from her attack. She'd done everything she could to stop the New Castle Killer during her time as sheriff, but it hadn't been good enough. Neither had running. Now a killer had wiped out her entire former team and turned his sights on her and Dylan. Because she'd been too weak to stop him. "I'm fine."

"You're biting the inside of your mouth again. I can confidently say that's not the case." The mattress dipped under his weight as Dylan settled on the edge. Rough fingers speared through her hair at the back of her neck and urged her to look at him. "I'm here. Whatever you need to feel, whatever you need to process, don't hold it in. It's only going to tear you apart."

"I can't." But those two small words weren't enough to protect herself from the flood raging forward. No matter how hard she tried to stay in control. Tears burned in her eyes, and she clung to Dylan's hand as hard as she could. He carefully tugged her upright into his chest, right over his heart, and…she shattered. "I can't let you die because of me."

DYLAN PUNCHED IN the code to the safe house door. The keypad beeped, the LED light blinked green and he pushed open the door. Shadows disappeared with a simple flick of the entryway light, and he motioned Remi past him inside. Mild concussion, twenty stitches in the back of her skull, even more in her side from the knife wound. She was lucky to be alive. If it hadn't been for her determination to fight back, he wasn't sure she would be, and damn, he admired the hell out of her for it. Not one of the investigators the killer had gone after had survived. No one but Remi.

"I'll clear the back rooms. You take the kitchen and office." She lowered her hand from her side as he closed the door behind them. Always the one to deny she was in pain, but Dylan knew the truth. She didn't wait for him to answer, disappearing down the hall.

He did a quick sweep of the areas he'd been assigned and met her back in the entryway. Scrapes, bruises and outright exhaustion marred her perfect features, and he wanted nothing more than to wrap his arms around her again. "I had Watson stock the fridge and pantry and set up the bedrooms while you were recovering in the hospital. Why don't you clean up while I cook something for us to eat?"

"What? You didn't like the peanut butter, jelly and nacho chip sandwiches?" A hint of a smile broke through the haunted emptiness in her features. Visibly fighting to stay steady on her feet, she shuffled back through the hallway toward the bedrooms. Three steps. Four. She stopped just past the office off to the left and turned her head over one shoulder, a shadow of the woman who'd led the Oregon division to the highest closing office in the country. "Thank you. For getting me out of there. I'm not sure I would've been able to find the exit to the lava tubes if you hadn't come for me."

The biological part of him wanted to close the short space between them, to help her forget everything she'd endured and to smooth the rough edges of the emotions that'd broken through to the surface in that hospital bed. Instead, he curled his fingers into the center of his palms to keep himself in place. "You were there for me when I needed you. It's about time I returned the favor."

Remi nodded once then continued down the hallway. A door clicked closed, and the sound of water hitting tile echoed through the house.

Dylan stared at the corner she'd vanished behind as his own pain reminded him a slug had been dug from his side less than twenty-four hours ago. The bullet itself had been sent to the forensics lab to see if it matched any other crimes in the database, but he didn't think anything significant would come back. Whoever'd abducted Remi had been too careful these past two years. He'd murdered twenty-six people before Watson had made a connection to the same killer. The bastard wasn't going to let a single bullet bring him down, and Dylan doubted the prints from Remi's phone would yield any useful results, either.

He dragged himself into the kitchen and wrenched open the oversize fridge to see what the former FBI bomb technician had stocked. The pain flared again. Nothing compared to the agony Remi had shouldered these past few hours after insisting she be discharged against doctor's orders. The doctor had sent her home with pain meds, but Dylan knew her. She'd only see the pills as a hindrance to solving the case.

Dylan pulled a fresh head of broccoli from one of the drawers, a bag of spinach, a cube of butter and sharp cheese from the fridge. He studied the selection of pasta in the pantry before choosing small shells for his plan. "Cheese solves everything."

He made quick work of shredding the block of cheese, poured a cup of milk and started boiling the pasta. Pure comfort food, and exactly what they both needed to get through the night. Mixing it all together in a single pot, he caught the sound of bare footsteps padding down the hallway. He took the homemade mac and cheese with broccoli and spinach off the stove and divided it between two large ceramic cereal bowls he'd found at the back of one of the cabinets. "Hope you're hungry."

He lifted his gaze to her and froze, pot in hand.

Lean muscle shaped curves along her calves and thighs below a pair of running shorts, and his mouth dried. The oversize T-shirt sponged water from her long, wet hair and did nothing to hide the outline of gauze underneath. Any thoughts he'd had of dinner instantly vanished. His gut flexed. Damn, she was beautiful, as though she'd been designed just for him.

"You're staring," she said.

"It's been so long since I've seen you in anything less than your standard uniform of long-sleeved shirts and boots. Can you blame me?" The heat from the pot registered, and Dylan tossed it onto the kitchen island. The loud reverberating sound of metal on granite shot through him. "Sorry. I… I didn't expect—"

"That I didn't sleep in my holster and Kevlar? I tried. It's not very comfortable. I had to settle for keeping my gun under my pillow and my vest beside the bed." A smile tugged at the edges of her mouth, and his heart jerked in his chest. When was the last time he'd seen her smile? Had he ever?

Her bare feet stuck to the hardwood slightly as she entered the kitchen. She pressed her hands into the granite, accentuating the long tendons in her forearms beneath the tattoos. The block letters branded across her forearm ended just above her wrist. "It smells good."

"The carbs and fats will help you recover faster, but veggies are an important food group." He pushed a bowl toward her and turned to extract two forks from one of the drawers. Handing one off to her, he dove into his own portion, and nearly melted in exhaustion right there in the middle of the floor.

"You seem to know your way around a kitchen. Why don't I remember that?" She forked a large bite into her mouth, careful of the split in her lip. A thin string of cheese flattened along her chin, and he reached up, slowly, to wipe it away. Her eyes widened as she stopped chewing, and the whole world seemed to stop right then.

Heat coiled through him as he envisioned closing that small distance between them, but Remi had made it clear before. Nothing would happen between them as long as they were working together, and he'd never been one to change the chief's mind. He forced himself to take a step back. "I don't think we got that far. You and I both know what we had in Delaware was nothing more than stress relief from the case. It worked. We didn't need much else."

"Is that what you really thought of us?" she asked. "That we were taking advantage of each other?"

"As far as I knew." Dylan took another bite to give himself long enough to process the change in her tone. One of the conditions she'd laid out when he'd joined her team of marshals had been to keep what'd happened between them in Delaware between them. There hadn't been any discussion, no hope of seeing if those passion-filled nights would lead to something more, and under no circumstances an encore. He set his bowl on the counter. "What would you call it?"

Remi stared at her dinner, pushing it around with the prongs of her fork. "I don't know. I guess I didn't realize you thought so low of me that you believed I could use you like that."

"I didn't see it as you using me, Sheriff." He shifted his weight between his feet, his serving of mac and cheese forgotten as the hurt in her voice resonated between them. "We both got what we wanted out of our arrangement, and you made it clear as soon as you'd left Delaware that we were through. I didn't automatically think because I came to Oregon that we would start up again."

"Are we through?" Her mouth parted as though she couldn't believe she'd said the words herself, and he froze in anticipation. “I know what I said when you signed on to work in my office. I know I’m your direct superior and anything unprofessional between us could lose us our jobs, but right now, Dylan, I need—”

He slid his hand behind her neck, pulled her into him and crushed his mouth to hers. Lightning struck behind his eyes as everything he’d fantasized about became reality. The kiss rocked him straight to his foundation, hungry, eager, desperate. A potent mixture of citrus body wash and Remi went straight to his head faster than the best-tasting whiskey and brought a low growl from his throat. He fit her against him, careful of their injuries, and deepened the kiss.

She arched into him, and every reason he shouldn’t push for something more between them evaporated. The investigation, the fact she’d become his chief deputy, the past—none of it mattered. Remi matched his fierce desperation. They’d denied themselves for so long, but damn it, he didn’t want to wait any longer. He couldn’t breathe, couldn’t think. There was only Remi.

She pressed her hand into his chest and increased the space between them, breaking the deliriously addictive desire twisting in his tender gut. Eyes closed, she settled back and smiled.

Opening her eyes, she pinned him with her bright blue gaze and fisted a handful of his shirt.

"What I was going to say was that I need you to forget our professional titles tonight and sit with me to keep me from falling asleep because of the concussion, but I can't say I didn't enjoy that."

"Oh, good. I was worried there for a minute you actually wanted me to kiss you." A laugh escaped up his throat as the truth of that statement burned between them, and he extracted his hand. Pulling the hem of her T-shirt in place, he leaned in close to whisper in her ear. "But remember, I let you go once, Sheriff. I'm not letting you get away a second time."

Chapter Ten

I'm not letting you get away a second time.

Moonlight beamed through the windows high above the large sectional she'd commandeered for the night. The light from the television cascaded around her, but she didn't care what program was on. Dylan's words still echoed in her head. As did the heart-pounding kiss he'd pulled her into in the kitchen. He'd taken lead in clearing the perimeter after he'd piled their dinner dishes into the sink, but the desire under her skin had yet to dissipate.

Remi studied the photos pinned to the makeshift board they'd created before the attack and brushed her finger against the pattern of scrapes across her knuckles. Dylan had saved her life. She'd been indebted to him the moment he'd pulled her from those caves. But if she was being honest with herself, kissing him back, letting him claim her from the inside, had nothing to do with repayment and everything to do with craving that human touch he'd offered. It'd been so long since she'd trusted someone the way she'd trusted him, and she hadn't been able to turn away. She hadn't wanted to turn away.

The front door sighed open, and the alarm panel on the wall beeped with two short bursts. Dylan's familiar footsteps echoed into the living room, but she still found herself sliding her hand around her sidearm beneath comforter that covered her. She'd been taken by surprise once and nearly died because of it. She wouldn't let it happen again. Familiar steel-gray eyes settled on her, and the pressure behind her sternum released.

"Perimeter's clear. No footprints in the mud. No fresh tire marks or evidence someone has come within two hundred feet of this place." He holstered his weapon at his hip and leaned against the wide opening between the entryway and the living room. He nodded toward her. "You moved the murder board in here."

Relief washed through her. No matter how long she'd stared at this board with their two suspects pinned in the center, she couldn't focus. Not on clearing the perimeter. Not on finishing her official statement to Gresham PD and Captain Paulson. Not on their next move. There was only Dylan. The private investigator who'd somehow managed to leave a piece of himself inside her before she'd left Delaware.

He'd been right earlier. What they'd had together had started as a conduit to release the stress of the New Castle case, but over a few short weeks had become something so much more. And that kiss… It hadn't merely been a biological reaction from adrenaline and danger. Not for her. It'd reminded her of everything she'd lost, everything she'd left behind. Everything she'd cared about. And it had changed everything. "I thought if I stared at our suspects' photos long enough, one of them would pipe up and tell me who killed Del Howe in that cabin."

"If they start talking, we're going to have to go back to the hospital." A warm, genuine smile tugged at one corner of Dylan's mouth as he stepped into the room. He unfastened his holster from his belt and set it on the end table. The couch dipped beneath his weight as he took up position beside her. Connected shoulder to hip, his proximity released a string of heat through her she'd denied existed these past six months. Until now. "How's the head?"

"Better than the stab wound." She arched her elbow over the back of the couch and turned into him. Suddenly the thin, oversize shirt and running shorts she'd donned after her shower left her lacking for a layer of physical protection between them. It left her feeling exposed, vulnerable, but if there was one thing in this psychotic mind game the killer had started she could count on, it was Dylan's integrity. He wouldn't hurt her.

She studied the shift of shadows down his face brought on by the television screen. Thick, dark hair curved along the angles of his jawline in perfect precision, and her skin tingled at the memory of his beard brushing against her chin and cheeks. "And the bullet hole in your side?"

He turned that compelling gaze onto her. "Medium-rare."

"You save lives. You know your way around a kitchen. You keep people awake so they don't die in their sleep." She lowered her hand to the back of his head and ran her fingers over his neck and shoulders. "I'm starting to think you should be the one wearing one of Reed's superhero T-shirts."

"Not people, Sheriff," he said. "Just you."

Her heart rate sped up, which she wasn't sure was a good thing considering the amount of force it'd taken to knock her unconscious. Remi slowed the trail she traced back and forth across his shoulder. "Why?"

"Why?" His expression matched the color of his eyes. Pure steel.

"You're one of the most stubborn, critical and idealistic investigators I've ever worked with. You keep to yourself, only speak when spoken to and you've made it a point to keep your distance between you and every one of your teammates in my division. Everyone except me." Her mouth dried as something inside reached for the hope she'd stashed at the back of her mind. "Why do you make an effort with me and no one else?"

Seconds passed, maybe a minute, and that same bit of hope she'd ignored all these years nearly suffocated her.

"I've spent most of my life getting lied to in one form or another. Before I became a private investigator and came to work with you on the New Castle Killer case, I'd lived in almost every state in the country by the time I was fifteen years old." Dylan directed his attention to the TV screen, his gaze distant. "My parents divorced when I was three, after my father found a letter from my mom at the top of her closet detailing how she was going to leave him. He confronted her about it. I remember a lot of screaming and the police showing up at our house. I was crying. I didn't know what was happening. But when it was over, my mother packed our bags and we got in the car. We never stopped driving. Not longer than a few months at a time. Whenever I asked her why I couldn't see my dad or why I had to change schools again, her answer was the same. 'So he can't find us.'"

A pit solidified in her stomach. "He was abusive?"

"That's the kicker. He never laid a hand on us. Turned out, she'd only wanted to leave him because of an affair she'd been having with one of the officers who'd come to the house that day. She lied to me about it for almost twenty years, tried to make me believe my father was the villain. That their marriage ended because of his selfishness and not hers." A humorless laugh escaped him. "She turned me against him, manipulated me to keep me under her control, and by the time I realized what'd happened, it was too late."

This wasn't the man who'd claimed her mouth with wild abandonment less than an hour ago. This wasn't the marshal she'd hired, or the private investigator she'd asked for help. All of that had been stripped away in an instant. All that was left was Dylan.

He faced her again, strong hands drawing her legs across his lap, and in that moment, she felt… herself. Not the chief deputy marshal she was supposed to be. It was him and her. No titles. No rules. Bare and exposed. She automatically reached for that emotional protection, the one thing she could use to reject others before they rejected her, but after what'd happened in those caves, she couldn't find it. There was nothing left.

"You're the only one who's never lied to me." He smoothed the pad of his thumb over her split lip. The salt from his fingers burned, but she didn't pull away. The resulting sting meant she was still here, still alive. He cocked his head to one side as another smile wiped the rigidity from his expression. "Well, at least not when it came to anything but your own well-being. Your honesty helps fight all the lies people have told me over the years, and being here with you… I'd give anything to hold on to this feeling of peace a little longer." He framed her jaw and pressed his forehead to hers as though he intended never to let her go. "I consider you exceptional, Remi. So I make an exceptional effort to be what you need me to be. Because you deserve nothing less."

"I don't deserve your admiration." Her exhale mixed with his in rapid bursts before Remi pulled away. Heat from his palm tunneled through bruised flesh, igniting the incessant need for her to be good enough, strong enough, to face the truth. He was more than the private investigator she'd hired in Delaware. He was more than the deputy she'd made part of her team. For her, he was everything she wanted to be. Rational, passionate, self-controlled. "I'm the one who got you into this mess. If I'd known there'd been a victim out there who'd survived, who'd target you—"

"No." Dylan shook his head, his hand moving to grip the back of her neck as he had in the kitchen but not in intimidation or dominance. In desperation. In need. "I watched you collapse into exhaustion at the end of every single day working the New Castle case. I saw how much you sacrificed to bring those victims home alive and stop Del Howe from killing again. You carried that entire investigation on your shoulders, and the men and women who worked beside you knew it. None of them would blame you if they were still alive, and neither do I. Not ever."

"You can't know that." The fight drained from her muscles, the past twelve hours since he'd pulled her from that cave catching up. "I'm the one who lost my job when we couldn't stop him. I was responsible."

"And yet I've never been so sure of anything in my life." His confidence melted into her, made her believe what he said was the truth. He loosened his grasp on her neck but didn't move to release her completely. He was giving her a choice. Keep running from the past—from him—or face it like the woman he believed her to be.

Remi didn't want to run anymore. Her breath caught in her throat as the answer she'd been hiding from all these years urged her to shove the comforter aside and slid her legs down his thighs. She wedged her knees into the back of the couch on either side of him, careful of their wounds. His fingers slid to her hips, holding her in place as she straddled him. Remi rested her hands on his shoulders and nearly pressed her mouth to his. "I hope you took one of your pain pills, Deputy Cove. I have a feeling this is going to hurt like hell."

FOOTSTEPS ECHOED down the hall, pulling Dylan from unconsciousness, before her perfect outline filled the door frame. Remi leaned against the wall as he fought to get balance. They'd somehow made it to one of the bedrooms last night after stripping each other bare on the living room couch. But he couldn't exactly remember how. A smile lit those iridescent blue eyes as morning sunlight streaked across the ceiling. "I was beginning to worry I'd knocked you out for good."

"Am I dead?" A jagged tear slit through the collar of her T-shirt. He remembered that part. After years of being deprived of her skin pressed against his, of her addictive taste in his mouth, he hadn't been able to wait. Her shirt had only gotten in the way.

Dylan dragged both hands across his face and pressed the heels of his palms into his eyes. Hell, he should've taken her up on her warning before she'd kissed him. He felt like he'd run a marathon with a bullet in his side. He pressed his hand into the corner of the gauze taped over his wound to get a better look at the damage. The gauze was dry, clean.

"Not quite." Offering him a steaming cup of coffee, she slid down onto the mattress as he pressed his back against the nearest wall. Bruises marred the smooth skin along her legs and knees, results of her fight with her attacker in the caves.

Remi took a sip from her mug and swallowed. "But I'm more than happy to try for a different result next time, if that's what you're aiming toward."

"Next time? Hell, I'm not even sure I've survived the first time." A laugh broke past the soreness in his chest as bone-deep satisfaction urged him to take her up on her challenge. He took the mug. Where were his clothes? "Did you…change my dressing while I was asleep?"

She hissed. "Yeah, sorry about that. After you fell asleep, I noticed you'd popped a couple stitches while we were…" Curling her fingers around her mug, she drew her gaze down the length of his chest and abdominals. "You were bleeding again, and I didn't want your wound to get infected, so I cleaned it and applied new gauze and tape."

"How?" he asked.

Her eyes suddenly diverted to an invisible speck of dust she swiped at with her free hand. "Let's just say I learned early on I could do anything I want to you after you fall asleep after sex."

Realization struck, and Dylan bolted upright. Coffee sloshed over his hand and stained the white sheets. He bit back the groan as pain exploded from his side and the coffee burned its way down the length of his forearm. A half dozen incidents rushed to the front of his mind. Kicking free from the sheets, he set the mug down and jumped to his feet. He pointed straight at her. "You. You're the reason I can't grow hair on this leg anymore, aren't you? You were shaving me while I was asleep."

"I have no idea what you're talking about." She took another sip of her coffee, every inch the chief deputy he'd come to admire over these past six months. Calm, confident and absolutely powerful. She was everything he wasn't and everything he hadn't realized he'd needed to keep his head on straight. "Besides, everyone knows once you start shaving, the hair comes back thicker and darker. You gotta wax if you want to keep that growth down."

"You were waxing me in Delaware?" Who the hell waxed another person while they slept? It took everything he had not to laugh while he stared at her. Two could play at this game. "You're going to pay for that, and I can think of plenty of ways to make sure you don't get away with it."

Eyes wide and innocent, Remi set her coffee on the floor and faced him, but he wasn't stupid enough to think he could best her mentally or physically. He had the weight, but she had the skill, even with a fresh stab wound in her side. "Innocent until proved guilty, Deputy. Didn't they teach you that at Glynco?"

"Funny how some of the hair started growing back after you took up with the marshals service." He threaded his hand around her waist and pulled her into his chest. Tipping her chin up, he brushed his mouth across hers in a teasing kiss that ignited only a hint of the desire they'd shared last night. With his luck, he'd be the one taking a cold shower, and she'd get away with making his leg itch for two months straight. Her body heat buried through the thin fabric of his boxers. "I think I'm going to have to start plotting my revenge."

"Like I said, I have no idea what you're talking about." Lifting onto her toes, she pressed her mouth against his and wrapped her arms around his neck. She arched into him, a low moan escaping her throat, and every inch of him caught fire. He'd lied to himself. Two couldn't play at this game, because the woman in his arms would win at every turn.

Remi stepped back, her fingers trailing down his chest until she slipped her hand into his for the briefest of moments. Crouching, she hefted her overnight bag over her shoulder, her mouth thinning into a line at the weight. "I'd be more than happy to help you even it out after we review statements from friends and family members of the two New Castle Killer victims. I've already run background checks, but it's possible someone knew their loved one survived the attack and has been helping him stay off law enforcement's radar all this time."

Dylan shook his head. No matter what'd she been through, how much pain she was in, Remi wouldn't stop. Not for her own health, and not at the expense of losing momentum in the case. He'd kept her awake for the recommended amount of time last night, but after that, she'd taken her well-being back into her own hands. The circles under her eyes had darkened since last night, and concern replaced the knot of desire coiling in his gut. He took a single step toward her. "You didn't sleep after you were cleared to, did you? You worked the case last night after we were finished."

Her smile slipped from her lips, and his nervous system kicked into overdrive. A single muscle in her jaw ticked. "I needed to know which one of them took me to that cave, which one of them has been killing my friends and coworkers for years without me knowing."

"You're biting the inside of your mouth," he said.

Her drawn inhale was a sign that she was ready for battle. The hard set of her mouth told him the passionate, vulnerable woman he'd gotten a glimpse of last night had only been temporary. This wasn't the sheriff he'd come to know, who'd practically admitted to waxing his leg for two months straight a few minutes ago. Squaring off with him, Chief Deputy Remington Barton leveled her chin with the floor. "In case I haven't made it clear for you, my sleeping habits don't fall under your purview of this case. We might have slept together last night, Deputy Cove, but I'm still your superior, and we have a murderer to find."

She turned from him and headed for the door.

"You see them when you close your eyes, don't you?" His instincts had confirmed the truth when he'd had to carry her to the bedroom two nights ago because she hadn't been able to function any longer. "You push yourself into exhaustion instead of taking the risk of falling asleep on your own. That way you don't have to see the faces of the victims we failed."

Remi froze, her head slightly turned over her shoulder. The small, shaved section at the back of her head revealed the stitches her surgeon had sutured less than eighteen hours ago. "You don't know what you're talking—"

"Yes, I do." Those same faces haunted him every night. "The men you have pinned to your board out there? They're the reason I started investigating the case on my own. They're the ones who pushed me to find the connection between the New Castle Killer and Del Howe." His pulse raced. "I'm the reason the son of a bitch got his hands on Tad Marrow, and the moment I heard the news, I swore I'd never let that happen to another victim."

"But I didn't," she said, so low he almost hadn't heard her.

"I know for a fact you did everything you could to stop Del Howe from killing again." He'd never been more sure of anything in his life. "Just like I know you're doing everything you can right now to bring his killer down. But that bastard almost took you from me, Sheriff. You were stabbed. He slammed your head through a window. At some point, your body isn't going to play by your rules anymore. You need to—"

"What do you mean he almost took me from you?" She faced him, and the strong, self-confident woman he'd worked with these past six months disappeared. In that moment, he envisioned her on the edge of a blade, trying to find balance between the mask she was compelled to wear in the line of duty and the woman underneath. Her mouth parted as she struggled to control the tremors in her hands, but she couldn't hide from him. Not anymore.

"We started sleeping together because we both needed the stress relief during the New Castle case, but that's not enough for me anymore," he said. "Not after what we've been through these past few months, and sure as hell not after what happened in those caves."

Resignation filtered through the slight ringing in his ears. He hadn't meant for the admission to slip out, but Remi was far too good of an investigator for him to hope she'd let this go. He took a step forward, then another, his gaze level with hers. "I want you, Remi. I've wanted you for a long time, and when that son of a bitch pointed his weapon at me, I knew not even a bullet was going to stop me from getting to you. Nothing would. You walked into my life because you were meant to be there, and I'm not ready to let you go."

Chapter Eleven

A quick hard thump in her chest was the only evidence she hadn't dreamed the conversation between her and Dylan. He wanted her. No hesitation. No mind games. Every aspect she'd fantasized about having after her entire family had been ripped from her in the flash of a faulty electrical outlet stood in front of her. But the sinking sensation of doubt kept her from accepting it as truth. No matter how many times she'd tried to convince herself otherwise, she couldn't change the fact Dylan Cove was tied to a past she'd tried to forget, a past she'd run from.

A combination of shame, guilt and the hefty burden of responsibility flooded through her. Dozens of family members had been counting on her to find the man who'd killed their loved ones. She'd let them all down. The people of New Castle County had made certain she'd paid the price for it, but the only way she'd been able to lead the Oregon division of US Marshals was to pretend losing her position as New Castle's sheriff hadn't affected her. Pretend that losing the job that was supposed to help her protect the people she'd served—to make up for not being able to protect her family—hadn't nearly killed her.

And Dylan… She cleared her throat. Dylan was a clear reminder she hadn't been good enough, that she might never be good enough. He hadn't realized it yet, but just as the citizens of New Castle had learned, it was only a matter of time before she disappointed him, too.

Remi took a deep breath, stretching the stitches in her side. "I need to check in with the ME concerning Howe's autopsy. With any luck, there's something there that might be able to tie us to which of his victims killed him."

Acceptance bled into the lines around his eyes, and her heart squeezed inside her chest. He wasn't going to push her on this. His tongue darted between his lips, resurrecting a flare of awareness in her lower abdominals. Ridges and valleys flexed across his midsection as he searched the bedroom floor. "I'll get dressed and get us some coffee. I can start going through the family background checks again as soon as I'm caffeinated."

"Good idea." Remi turned, heading for the bedroom door. She had to focus on the case, had to stop a killer from exacting his revenge.

"You can't run forever, Sheriff," he said, and she leaned her weight against the closed bathroom door, hand on the knob. "Sooner or later, you're going to realize you deserve to move on from what happened in Delaware, and when you do, I'll be there. Waiting."

She turned the doorknob and fell inside the modern, renovated bathroom. Instant exhaustion claimed the muscles in her legs. Remi closed the door behind her before she sank to the cold penny tile. A long vanity with white cabinetry and matching granite led to a large glass shower at the other end of the room.

The subtle hint of Dylan's aftershave tickled the back of her throat as she begged the last remnants of energy in her body to be enough to get her across the tile, but he'd been right. There was always a point where her body wouldn't play by her rules anymore. She'd been able to push herself this long, but time had finally run out. She couldn't go any farther. She'd lost too much blood, used too much adrenaline and had hit her head too hard. She had nothing left to give to this case or to Dylan. She battled to keep her eyes open, barely aware of the brush of cool air along her legs.

She heard footsteps, then rushing water, but she couldn't open her eyes. Strong, familiar arms threaded under the backs of her knees and lifted her against a wall of bare muscle.

"I've got you, Sheriff." His voice soothed the aches, the pain, the fear. Dylan. "You are the most frustrating woman I've ever met in my life, but no matter how many times you deny there's more between us than a professional relationship, I know the truth. I can feel it, and I know you do, too. Otherwise, I think you would've already tried to shoot me for coming in here."

Cold raced along the bottoms of her feet as he righted her and tightened his grip around her waist to hold her against him. Tearing fabric reached her ears before warm steam caressed her skin. He'd ripped her shirt from her body, finishing the job he'd started last night. Her running shorts pooled at her ankles, and he maneuvered her beneath the warm shower spray.

"Come on, Remi. Hold on to me." He hauled her arms over his shoulders, not letting her go for a second.

She'd been too tired, too…broken to make it on her own, but he'd gotten her the rest of the way. Dylan slid his arms around her, her head resting against his shoulder. Prickling heat pounded into her back. He trailed casual circles between her shoulder blades, and she summoned the energy to cling to him as much as she could. She wouldn't have made it out of that damn cave without him, wouldn't have been able to work this case without him by her side. He'd believed her when she'd said she hadn't killed Del Howe, and that counted for more than she could ever admit. The isolated, critical deputy trusted her. He made an effort with her. He cared about her. And she… Damn it. She'd started falling for him.

Remi forced her eyes open, aware of the material scratching the skin of her thighs. "You're wearing jeans."

"I was getting dressed when I realized you hadn't turned on the water to the shower." The rich timbre of his voice, combined with the circles he pressed into her back, worked to clear the exhausted haze from her head. "My instincts were right. You need me. I hope you don't drive when you're this tired."

"I hope you don't…" The sharp scent of citrus dove into her lungs before soft strokes and bubbles tickled the sensitive skin down her spine. "I don't remember what I was going to say."

"You're delirious and on the verge of another collapse," he said.

She closed her eyes, indulging in the sound of his laughter. Tough calluses caught on her skin as Dylan ran the bodywash the length of her arms, across her chest and down the other side. In minutes, he'd washed away the blood, dirt and post sex residue, handling her as though she were made of glass. Leaving her to stand on her own, he peeled the gauze from her side and surveyed the damage underneath. “We need to get your wound cleaned up and put you into bed. I’ll keep working the case while you rest.”

“You…deserve better.” She hadn’t meant to say the words, but she’d never been more confident of anything in her life. Even now, as a killer closed in around them, he was taking the time to care for her. To make sure she got through the next day, the next hour, the next minute. He’d lost as much as she had when she’d been fired from the sheriff’s department, but he’d never blamed her. Not once. “You were the best…investigator I’d worked with in Delaware. That’s why…when you applied to the marshals, I made sure you ended up in Oregon. I told all the division heads you were mine. I told them they had to turn you down for the open positions in their offices, but now I know I’m never going to be…good enough for you.”

“You made sure I didn’t get any of those jobs so I would have to come to Oregon?” Dylan dipped his chin to his chest. His hands hesitated above her ankles; his touch was so light, she barely felt it.

She latched onto his shoulders for balance, and a sharp sense of clarity rippled through her, but it was too late. The truth settled between them as he straightened, and there was nothing she could do to take it back, to make what she’d done okay. Remi couldn’t read his expression, and a knot of fear coiled deep in her belly. She tried to shake the exhaustion, but it was only a matter of time before she collapsed. "Dylan, I'm sorry. I… I didn't mean—"

"Didn't mean to admit you like me more than you've let on?" He hung the loofa from the shower nozzle and twisted the water off. Echoes of dripping water attacked the nerves lining her skin with each splash from the showerhead. He reached for one of the soft, white robes hanging on the wall beside the shower and wrapped it around her, clenching the collar around her neck. "You've been holding out on me, Sheriff."

She didn't know what to say to that. She threaded her arms into the sleeves and let him loosely secure the tie at her waist. Within minutes, cool air brushed against her collarbone as he led her back to the bedroom they'd ended up in for the night, but it did nothing to douse the newfound admiration swirling through her.

She followed his lead and fell back on the bed, her eyes heavier than ever before. Modern angles sloped from the ceiling above, casting shadows across his handsome face. She framed one side of his jaw, stubble prickling her warm skin. Her hand fell back to her chest. "You're not angry… I might've limited your career opportunities?"

"To be honest, I'm a little surprised you let it slip at all, even as tired as you are." Leaning over her, Dylan pressed a light kiss to her mouth and pulled back. Of all the times her body had shut down, she'd made sure no one would be there to take advantage of her at her lowest, but she trusted him. "I know exactly where I want to be, Remi, and right now, that's with you."

ANOTHER USELESS LEAD.

"Damn it." Dylan tossed the file across the kitchen table and rubbed at his eyes. He'd gone through every family member, coworker, friend, former lover and acquaintance on file for each of the New Castle Killer's victims. No evidence these people had any clue one of their loved ones had survived. No large debts or sudden absences from work. It'd take a warrant to get phone records and data from their personal computers, but his instincts said if one of Del Howe's victims had survived and become a killer, their family and friends had no idea.

If it hadn't been for the fact Remi had noted the scars on her attacker's hand, Dylan would've doubled down on the involvement of their first suspect. Sergeant Daniel Nguyen still had the means and the motive, despite his shift schedule and the fact he'd been in the interrogation room when Remi had been abducted confirmed he wasn't the killer they were looking for. As of right now, the Gresham PD officer was only guilty of planning to kill Del Howe. The man who'd given the

New Castle Killer a taste of his own medicine was still out there.

"Good…morning?" Remi headed for the coffee maker, no signs of exhaustion in her movements, and a tightness seized the space around his heart. Long-sleeved shirt, cargo pants, weapon holstered, hair pulled away from her face. Damn, the woman bounced back like no one he'd known. She glanced at the clock on the microwave as she reached for a mug. "Not morning. Good afternoon."

"You don't look like you're going to pass out anymore." He pressed his forearms onto the kitchen table to stay focused on the case files in front of him and not on the way the lean muscles of her arms flexed as she poured herself a cup of coffee. "That's an improvement."

"Tell anyone what happened, and I'll do more to you than wax that leg while you're asleep. And thank you." Silence settled between them as appreciation brightened her eyes, and Dylan nodded. She riffled through the pantry until she found a box of granola bars and crossed the kitchen with her bounty in hand. Her smile punched him straight in the gut. Taking her seat, she quickly discarded the wrapper around her on-the-go meal and studied the papers spread across the table's surface. "How far have you gotten with the family background checks?"

"Just finished. There's nothing here." He leaned

back in his chair, memorizing the way her eyes darted across the files in rapid succession as though she only needed a split second to review the text. He nodded at the murder board to his left. "If our killer is one of these men, as we suspect, he's doing a damn fine job of making sure we don't find him."

Her voice hollowed, her gaze distant. "The man in that cave told me Del Howe had awakened something inside him the day he was attacked. Something like the New Castle Killer had showed him who he really was. Our suspect hadn't ever killed before he set his sights on the investigating team working the case, but now he can't seem to stop. Even if he manages to kill us, I don't think he'll ever be finished. He's come too far to stop now." She swallowed a chunk of her granola bar and tossed the rest onto the table, seemingly losing her appetite. "Have you checked hospital records for the type of injuries Howe's victims sustained?"

"I ran the parameters through the system, but there were no hits on any patients suffering knife wounds around the time our victims were reported missing. Nothing came up under any of their names, either. Our guy might never have visited a hospital after escaping his captor, or—"

"Or he lied about how he sustained the injuries and gave a false name when he checked in." Remi shuffled through the reports, iridescent blue eyes lighter than he'd seen in days. Her split lip wasn't as swollen, the bruising already turning blue on her jaw. She flipped through page after page of background information he'd gathered. "Makes sense. If he was scared Howe would come for him again to finish what he started, the victim would've done anything to make sure the New Castle Killer couldn't locate him."

"Victim implies innocence." Dylan pushed back his chair and stretched the stiffness from his neck and shoulders. The sting of tape pulling at the fine hairs across his side brought total awareness to the pain he'd ignored the past six hours while Remi had slept. "Whoever stabbed you and put a bullet in my side has killed twenty-six people that we know of. Not sure we should keep calling him a victim."

"Then I vote we call them Killer One and Killer Two to keep things from getting confusing." Her wide smile pierced straight through the lethargy closing in. She set the files down and stared at them. "There are so many moving pieces to this case. Some of which we can't even see yet. Is there any mac and cheese left over from the other night?"

"Fridge." Dylan set his palms onto the edge of the table. They were still waiting for ballistics to match the bullet from her abductor's gun to other crimes and to see if the forensics lab could pull prints from Remi's phone. But Dylan didn't have much hope. Their suspect had ensured none of the murders could forensically be connected to one another or to him. He was methodical, calculated and more dangerous than any fugitive he'd ever chased. "Why did you want me in Oregon?"

Remi pulled the large container with their unfinished meal from the depths of the fridge and froze for the briefest of moments. "I was hoping me telling you what I'd done was part of a bad dream. Then I remembered I go out of my way to make sure I don't have dreams."

She set the container on the counter and made quick work of prying the lid free. "I investigated you before I hired you to work the New Castle case with the department. I wanted to make sure nothing could come back and bite me in the ass down the line. One of your past cases, the disappearance of a four-year-old boy, was what made my decision for me. The family was unloading groceries. When they turned back around, the boy had disappeared off their driveway. No one could find him, not even local police, so his parents hired you."

He remembered the case, one of his first, but while he'd known she'd had to pitch his coming on the case to the people of New Castle County, he hadn't realized she'd looked that far back into his career.

"The police I questioned said you were out in

the field every day and late into the night, looking for him. Nearby parks, neighborhood pools, the fields around his house. When that wasn't enough, you re-interviewed everyone the cops had taken statements from until you realized he hadn't left his neighborhood at all."

She scooped a spoonful of cold mac and cheese into her mouth and turned stark blue eyes onto him. "One of the neighbors had recently lost her grandson, about the same age as the boy you were looking for, and she was suffering from Alzheimer's. She'd taken him home, thinking he was her grandson come to visit her. No one else had even considered the possibility. That's when I knew I wanted you working the case. You were the kind of investigator who wouldn't stop looking until you'd recovered the victims or brought down the killer, no matter how many obstacles got in your way. So when I lost my job as sheriff, and I came to work for the marshals…you were my first thought. You're always my first thought."

He didn't know what to say to that, what to think.

Her phone vibrated on the surface of the island, and she reached for it. Sliding her thumb across the screen, Remi let the softness leave her voice as she answered. "Tell me you have something good, Foster."

Dylan turned back to the paperwork spread

across the kitchen table. There had to be something there—anything—that would lead them to the man who'd killed twenty-six people over the past two years and abducted Remi straight from the Gresham PD station. Surveillance footage hadn't done them a damn bit of good. The perp had been wearing a ski mask.

The men the New Castle Killer murdered weren't professionals. Tony Rasmussen had worked for his father's printing shop before his body had turned up in an alley behind his apartment building. He wasn't their killer. Brett Smith had been studying programming to become a video game designer, and although his body hadn't been recovered, there'd been too much blood left at the scene for the medical examiner to rule anything but murder.

As for Tad Marrow, the veterinarian's assistant had been loved by everyone he'd come into contact with and even went as far as to volunteer at the local homeless shelter. Law enforcement had looked for his remains for two months before the ME had officially declared the victim dead, but once again, the amount of blood… Dylan recalled the crime scene photos. No one could've survived that attack, but neither of their remaining suspects had the skills or the psychological profile of a serial killer hiding the fact he was actually alive all this time. "Except he'd said the New Castle Killer had awakened something in him that day."

Remi's low voice tendrilled through the sudden haze of inspiration.

He leaned forward in his chair and tilted the laptop screen closer. None of the background information, profiles and character statements were doing them a damn bit of good because the men who'd been attacked didn't exist anymore. Not psychologically. They'd been working off the assumption the victims would be the same men coming out the other side of a knife, but trauma had a way of changing people. Damn it. Dylan should've seen it before now.

A rush of adrenaline burned in his veins as he logged into the Warrant Information Network federal database. The information he needed didn't fall under the normal purview of his job as a deputy US marshal. Law enforcement operations, fugitive investigations, warrant administration, threat management, witness security protocols, district investigations—none of that would help him right now but the network did give him access to the National Crime Information Center.

"That was Foster. He said Del Howe's autopsy report was finalized an hour ago." Remi closed the distance between her and where he sat at the kitchen table, her voice more tense than a few minutes ago.

Dylan pulled back from the laptop. He didn't look at her, couldn't. He knew it would've been only a matter of time before the truth came to light. He'd tried to warn her before they'd taken on the case, but now, everything he'd worked for these past three years would tell her exactly what kind of man she'd let into her office, into her bed.

Remi tossed her phone onto the table in front of him, the report on her screen. "You lied to me."

Chapter Twelve

Falling in love was like handing someone a gun pointed at her heart and hoping they'd never pull the trigger.

Dylan had pulled the trigger.

Bits of conversation, whispered secrets and addictive kisses buzzed in her head from the past few days. Over and over, she'd ignored her instincts to keep her emotions locked behind the armor she'd spent most of her life constructing, and now she had to face the consequences. "You told me you'd only been to Del Howe's cabin once, with permission from the owners and a key to get inside while he was off the premises. But this report details a sample of dried blood that matches your DNA embedded in a wound on the back of his left hand."

She tried to keep herself from jumping to conclusions, but DNA didn't lie. Curling her fingers into the centers of her palms, Remi battled to control the tremors fighting up her arms as every minute of the past three days came into question. She'd brought Dylan Cove into her office, depended on him with sensitive material for his investigations, let him into her bed and into her heart, and he'd lied to her.

Color drained from Dylan's face, his body tensing as though considering his options, but there was no point in denying it. "You're right. I lied."

An invisible earthquake rocked through her, and she fought the urge to reach out for the chair. Pure, unadulterated anger exploded in her chest as the pieces of the puzzle she'd been more than willing to ignore from the beginning fit together. "You figured out who the New Castle Killer was, and you trailed his movements from Delaware to Oregon. You used your position as a US marshal to convince the owners of the cabin to let you search the place, but Howe must've come back to the property."

He pushed away from the table, stood and faced her. Regret played across his handsome features, but it wouldn't save him now. "Remi—"

"The DNA the ME recovered from the body was embedded in a wound across the bridge of Del Howe's knuckles, Cove." Emotional self-preservation arced through her, and she increased the space between them. Her weapon weighed heavy in her holster, but she hoped to hell he wouldn't make her pull it. "You found the man responsible for killing three victims in New Castle, and you couldn't let him get away with what he'd done. Just as you couldn't stop looking for that boy all those years ago. Only instead of arresting him, you confronted him."

"You're damn right, I did." A hardness she'd never experienced transformed his expression the moment she'd called him by his last name, and the light she'd come to crave in his gaze died. His attention dipped to her sidearm. "Everything you've said up until now is true. He came back before I finished searching the property, but I'd already found his closet of surveillance photos. He walked through the door, and all I saw was a man who'd targeted the one person I couldn't stand to lose. You.

"We fought. He must've gotten a good hit in for that much DNA to be left in his knuckles. After I overpowered him, I warned him I'd kill him if anything happened to you, but I left the son of a bitch alive when I walked out of that house." He raised his eyes to hers. "Don't hold back on my account, Chief. You were on a roll."

This wasn't the man she'd come to know over these past few days, the one who'd made her mac and cheese, pulled her off the bathroom floor when she hadn't been able to function and showed her passion beyond her wildest dreams. In that moment, she didn't recognize the deputy she'd fallen for at all. Battle-ready tension wound through her. She wouldn't reach for her weapon. Not unless Cove gave her a reason. She'd dealt with criminals every day on the job, but she'd never suspected one of her own.

"Go on, boss. We both know where you're going with this. Say it." He took a step toward her, and her fingers tingled for the warmth of steel in her grip. The small muscles in his jaw flexed under pressure, sharpening the angles of his cheekbones. "Accuse me of being the one who gave that bastard everything he deserved."

"I can't. There's not enough evidence to prove what happened between you and Del Howe didn't happen before his murder or resulted in his death. Yet." A coldness swept through her as her conversation with Deputy Beckett Foster replayed in her head, and a small bit of emotional control returned. Dylan seemed to relax a fraction, shifting his weight between both legs as she came to terms with the real reason he'd accepted her offer to work in Oregon. "But Gresham PD was able to obtain a warrant using that sample to search your apartment."

Physical pain bolted through her side as she struggled to keep her voice steady. "They found your case files on the New Castle Killer. They can prove you've been using USMS resources to investigate Del Howe the moment you graduated from

Glynco. That's why you applied for the marshals service and accepted my offer to work in the Oregon division, isn't it? Not for the chance you and I'd be working together again, but because you were using me and this job to find him. You knew what you were doing. You knew it would hurt me, but somehow that didn't stop you."

The truth pushed through the cracks in her armor and destroyed everything in its path. Her eyes burned, but she wouldn't let the tears fall. Not here. Not now.

"Am I under arrest?" The veins bulged in his arms.

"No. If it weren't for you and your obsession with the case, we never would've connected Del Howe as the New Castle Killer." She swallowed past the thickness in her throat but couldn't stop the pain from spreading. "But as of this moment, you are suspended without pay until Gresham PD's investigation is complete."

Surprise softened the edges of his expression. "Remi, don't do this—"

"You lied to me!" She forced herself to take a deep breath, but she'd already reached her breaking point. "You used my team, you used me, and now Gresham PD has made you their lead suspect in Del Howe's murder. I can't trust you."

She pulled her shoulders back, drawing on the same strength that'd gotten her through the worst years of her life after her family had died. "Dylan Cove, you're required to turn in your badge, your weapon and any additional notes you've collected during the case while Gresham PD continues to investigate Del Howe's murder."

He'd lied to her, lied to the team, lied to the police. While his actions had resulted in answering critical questions in the New Castle case, Remi couldn't trust him. Not on her team, and not with her heart. Heat burned up her neck as he solemnly nodded his acceptance of the web he'd caught himself in.

"It was a pleasure, Chief Barton. Every minute." Turning toward the kitchen table, he unholstered his weapon, released the magazine, cleared the chamber and set everything on the table. Cove unclipped his badge from his belt, stared down at it before he placed it beside his sidearm, and her heart shot into her throat. "Who knows? Maybe this isn't the end."

He crossed the room and rounded into the hallway leading to the front door. One breath. Two. Two beeps of the alarm announced his exit.

She forced one foot in front of the other, her legs heavy with grief, disbelief, betrayal. It wasn't the fact that Dylan had been at the cabin. He'd been honest enough at the beginning of this investigation she'd known there was a possibility Forensics would come back on him. It was that he'd lied to her about confronting Del Howe. Not only that, he'd used her move into the US Marshals Service to advance his own agenda, and he dragged her and her team into the conspiracy. The killer hadn't left behind much evidence, but now the DNA embedded in the victim's knuckles proved Dylan had been in that cabin, that he'd struggled with the New Castle Killer. It was only a matter of time before the FBI implicated the rest of the Oregon division.

Remi punched in the code on the alarm panel at the door and armed the system, but her internal walls were already crumbling. From the moment he'd walked through the front door three nights ago, Dylan had chipped at the edges of her armor while simultaneously making her feel as though she had control. The sandwiches, the kisses, the way he'd held her in the shower. It had all been a lie. A ploy to obtain her trust and the resources she commanded. And it had worked. She'd actually believed there could've been more to them than the occasional stress relief. She'd believed she was enough. For him, for the victims of their investigations, for the witnesses they'd been assigned to protect.

Tears trailed down her cheeks. "None of it was real." The words took shape, became real. She didn't love him. How could she love someone who'd never really existed?

Turning back to the living room, she fought against the ache in the center of her chest. The pain in her side extended across her midsection, and Remi collapsed into the side of the bookcase. The books toppled one after the other onto the floor at her feet. She closed her eyes against the oncoming dizziness, but it never surfaced. No. This wasn't the familiar gnaw of exhaustion or the loss of adrenaline leaving her empty. A gut-wrenching nausea stole the air from her lungs.

A sob escaped up her throat, and suddenly she was back in that cave, desperate for a single molecule of light to cut through the darkness. She pressed her fingers into the smooth wood, but in her mind, it was as coarse as thousands of tons of rock holding her prisoner, and Remi found herself completely and utterly alone. She heard nothing but the sound of her own breathing, and she hurt at the thought of never seeing the man who'd pulled her from the strangling grip of the past.

It was dark. It was cold. It was lonely.

Only, no one was coming to save her this time.

HE'D BECOME A SUSPECT.

Dirt and gravel crunched under his boots as he headed toward his SUV. He'd known it would've only been a matter of time. It'd been impossible for him to ensure he hadn't left any trace inside

Howe's cabin after the struggle, but he'd left the killer alive and breathing. Bloody, but alive.

Dylan wrenched the driver's-side door open and hauled himself inside. Studying the shadows creeping across the main window, he tried to make out movement on the other side of the glass, but he knew better. Remi wouldn't make herself a target by standing in front of the damn window. She was too smart for that.

Hell, there was no way to prove he hadn't been the one to kill the New Castle Killer without more evidence, especially without DNA tying another suspect to the murder. But that didn't compare to the betrayal he'd witnessed in Remi's features when she'd put his motive together.

Remi had been right. The notes he'd kept in his apartment, the surveillance photos he'd taken of Howe over the past year—he'd used her and her position within the marshals service to track the serial killer they hadn't been able to apprehend in Delaware.

While he'd convinced himself his reasons had been justified at the time, he felt as though he was treading water as the hollowness in his chest grew more determined to pull him under. Because this time, his choices had put more than one life at risk. This wasn't about catching one killer anymore. This was about keeping Remi alive.

He considered turning back, but Dylan started

the vehicle and put the safe house and Remi in the rearview mirror. He'd made a mistake by not listening to Tad Marrow all those years ago. He wasn't going to let this mistake define the rest of his life. Not when he could do something about it.

Suburban houses blurred in his vision as he sped across downtown Gresham. The hikers who'd claimed they'd noticed Howe's body through the window had lied. If he tracked down the woman—Annabell Ross—to get a description of her hiking partner that day, he might be able to narrow down which of the New Castle Killer's victims had attacked Remi or eliminate them from suspicion completely. Only trouble was finding her. Gresham PD hadn't been able to make contact after the duo had given their statements. No answer on her cell phone. No response at her residence. They hadn't been able to enter without a warrant, permission or signs of a struggle, but that didn't mean Annabell couldn't help.

The pain in his side flared as he filled his lungs. No amount of calm breaths would settle the pounding of his pulse behind his ears. Not when the cracks in Remi's expression after she'd learned the truth replayed over and over in his head.

Now I know I'm never going to be...good enough for you. Her slurred confession undid him, and he strengthened his hand on the steering wheel. Wasn't good enough for him? Hell, Remington Barton was better than he could ever be. She challenged him. Gave his life meaning. She exemplified strength. And he'd hurt her. Worse. He'd betrayed her after she'd trusted him with her deepest vulnerabilities and let him see her at her weakest. He pressed his free hand down his face. She was the best investigator he'd had the pleasure of working with, and he'd taken advantage of her for his own revenge. Not good enough for him? That wasn't possible. Remi was everything to him. "Damn it."

He'd fix this. He'd find the missing hiker to get more information on her partner, and he'd end the sick game closing in around them. At least then, Remi would be safe. He followed the GPS on his phone to the address given by the witness in her statement to Gresham PD and pulled up in front of the house when his phone chirped with his arrival.

A sprinkling of hot summer rain streaked down the passenger-side window as he surveyed the witness's property. The ranch-style, light blue home stood out among the others in the neighborhood, its cheery bright yellow door hung with a wreath. The well-manicured lawn and flowerbeds had been kept in pristine shape. That, combined with his knowledge that Annabell Ross obviously enjoyed the outdoors, had led Dylan to believe the owner took great care of nature and went out of her way to preserve it. The recycle bin positioned near the garage only added to her profile point.

Dylan turned off the engine and reached for the glove box. Remi had taken his duty weapon back at the safe house, but it wasn't his only firearm. Holstering the 9mm Smith & Wesson, he shouldered out of the vehicle. The rain was starting to pick up as he headed up the driveway. Corner lot, exposed to the street from the south and west, fence to the east between Annabell's home and the neighbors, trees in the backyard. Good location. A lot of vantage points.

He hit the front porch and rang the doorbell once followed by quick knocks to ensure she'd heard him. Seconds ticked by, a minute. No answer. "Annabell Ross, it's Deputy—" No. He wasn't a marshal anymore. "It's Dylan Cove. I was one of the officers at the scene a few days ago. Wonder if I might ask you some questions."

The rain picked up, as though sensing the distress coiling in his gut. Gresham PD had advised Ms. Ross to stay in touch until they concluded their investigation into Del Howe's death. Apparently, her respect for the community didn't extend to those responsible for keeping it safe. He hopped off the cement porch and peered through the nearest pane of a small bay window. White curtains shifted inside, blowing this way and that with the help of what looked like an overhead fan.

He shielded his eyes from the glare of a nearby streetlamp to get a better look inside. Conservationists didn't usually leave their fans on when they were away. Minimalist furniture and décor had been expertly placed throughout the living room and dining room. No television. No personal effects aside from a few photos on a bookshelf in the back. His heels sank into the soil as he repositioned himself for a better view. This was a woman who could pick up and go at a moment's notice. Hell, maybe she had just gone on another adventure with her small group of cavers as Captain Paulson believed. But his instincts told him if Annabell's hiking partner had been the one to kill Del Howe as the evidence suggested, then she hadn't lived long after giving her statement.

Dylan followed the flowerbed around the side of the house, senses at an all-time high. Water fell from his hair and collected around his collar. The backyard was as well manicured as the front. Healthy grass, fresh flowers, a large line of trees leading into pure wilderness beyond the property line. Old wood protested under his weight as he climbed the back stairs and tried the sliding-glass door. The heavy pane screeched along the track. He froze, holding his breath. "Annabell?"

No answer.

His pulse slammed wildly at the base of his neck as he stepped over the threshold into the galley kitchen. Builder's grade wood cabinets, a large white fridge, stainless-steel stove. Not much clutter on the counters. Peeling linoleum threatened to trip him up from nearly every angle. A small round table with four chairs took up space on his other side. Three large arches led into the living room at the front of the house and the front door, a hallway off to his left. Presumably to the bedrooms. No stairs as far as he could tell.

"Ms. Ross?" He freed his weapon, his finger stilled on the trigger. He wasn't sure what he'd expected to find, but the compulsion that'd pushed him to finish what he'd started with the New Castle Killer directed him down the hallway. Something wasn't right here. He nudged open the first door with the toe of his boot. A bathroom. Clear. He turned the knob of the door across the hallway and hit the lights. A single twin-size bed sat in the center of the room. No other furniture. Dread pooled at the base of his spine as he caught hints of a foul odor. He moved forward to the last bedroom. Hand on the doorknob, Dylan braced himself against the hollow wood.

Decomposition.

Covering his nose and mouth with his gun hand, he forced his way inside and turned on the lights. Wide brown eyes stared at him from Annabell's upside-down position over the edge of the bed. Discolored bruising and angry inflammation circled her neck, her skin ashen white compared to the last time he'd seen her. "Son of a bitch."

The hiking partner. Henry Sallow. He'd used her as an alibi that day near Del Howe's cabin, pretended he'd found the body instead of being the one responsible for the New Castle Killer's death, and discarded Annabell when he was finished with her. Dylan hadn't been fast enough.

Damn it. He had to call it in, had to let Remi know. He holstered his weapon. Unpocketing his phone, he hit the speed dial for her cell and hoped to hell she'd answer. This wasn't about what'd happened between them. This was another murder in the wake of twenty-six others. The line rang once. Twice.

Dylan turned back toward the hallway, but a bolt of pain shot through his chest, along his arms and into his legs. The phone fell from his grasp and bounced off the carpet. The outline of the attacker blurred in his vision as two electric nodes forced high doses of amps through his body. His hands automatically fisted as he swung out, but he met nothing but air just before he hit the floor.

Unending pain coursed through him as his attacker stepped into the light, Dylan's arms and legs jerking without his permission. Remi had been right. His throat convulsed around the only word he could get out of his mouth. "You."

"Hello, Cove." His attacker reached down and ended the call on Dylan's phone. "I told I wouldn't forget about you."

Chapter Thirteen

"Cove!" Remi pressed the phone to her ear, but there wasn't any response. No, no, no, no. Glancing at the screen, she realized the call had ended. *Hello, Cove.* She'd recognized that voice, the one that'd embedded in her head the moment she'd heard it in the caves. The killer had found him.

She slapped her hand over Dylan's badge and weapon to collect them from where he'd set them on the table and charged for the front door. After disarming the alarm, she fisted her keys and ran for her vehicle. The killer was trying to finish what he'd started. She hauled herself in behind the steering wheel and stored Dylan's weapon in the center console. Fishtailing away from the safe house, Remi pushed her hair out of her face and dialed the first number that came to mind.

Ringing filled the SUV's cabin through the speaker system. "Foster."

"Cove is in trouble. I need you to find him."

Emotional rawness in her voice revealed the personal nature between her and the deputy she'd fallen for, but Remi didn't have time to consider the consequences of that right now. Dylan wasn't an active member of her team any longer, but she wasn't going to let him become the next victim.

"Last known location?" Deputy Beckett Foster retained the highest fugitive recovery rate in the country. With a former conman for a father and a falsely accused fugitive who'd mothered his child, the marshal dedicated every instinct and resource he had to finding the people he'd been assigned. No matter the situation.

Now she needed him to use those same skills in her favor. Hesitation tightened the cords in her throat. The team had known she'd been working out of the Gresham safe house, but they hadn't known Dylan had been staying there with her. She licked her lips, glancing into the rearview mirror as desperation tore through her chest. "The safe house outside of Gresham."

"How long ago?" Foster hadn't missed a beat. If he'd suspected an interpersonal relationship between his chief deputy and another marshal, his voice hadn't revealed it.

Leather groaned under her fingers as she wedged her grip around the steering wheel. "He called me seven minutes ago, but the line cut off. I recognized the killer's voice on the other end. It's the same man who took me from the Gresham PD parking lot. I'm sure of it."

"Tracking Cove's phone now." Clicks from a keyboard filtered through the line, keeping in time with her pulse. "The phone has either been turned off or the SIM card removed to keep me from tracking it, but his last call came from a house on the east side of the city belonging to an Annabell Ross."

She knew that name. "That's the witness from Del Howe's crime scene. Gresham PD has been trying to get in touch with her for follow-up questions after she and her hiking partner discovered the body." Realization struck, and Remi pressed the back of her skull into the seat. "Cove said preliminary reports showed traces of volcanic rock in the footprints that led up to the cabin window, right?"

"According to Reed, that's how Cove was able to narrow your location after you'd been abducted. He added the male witness…a guy named—" papers rustled in the background "—Henry Sallow—as a possible suspect, but police haven't been able to find anything on him, either."

"That's because he doesn't exist. Inform Gresham PD we have reason to believe Del Howe's killer is at that address." Damn it. She'd practically accused Dylan of being involved in Howe's death, and he'd run straight to the only person who could prove someone else had been there that day. She'd suspended him, taken his weapon and destroyed every reason for him to back away from the case. "Forensic evidence placed Deputy Cove at the death scene prior to Howe's murder. He must've gone there to dig up more information to prove he wasn't the killer."

Foster's doubt pierced through the line. "Chief..."

"I already know what you're going to say, Foster. Because I've told myself over and over that I have to keep my personal opinions and feelings out of this case, but no matter how many times I try to tell myself otherwise, this case is personal. It has been since I left Delaware."

Gresham city streets streaked in her peripheral vision as she pressed her toes into the accelerator. "Cove told me when Del Howe's body was first discovered that he'd been in the house with permission from the owners, but the report... The report showed he'd confronted Howe, and Gresham PD can prove he's been using USMS resources to continue the investigation into the New Castle Killer case. Cove's DNA was found inside the lacerations on Howe's knuckles, which most likely came from a struggle between them, as he claimed."

"You believe him?" Foster asked.

The deputy's question echoed inside her head until the words blurred together into incoherent nonsense and mixed with the events of the past three days. Dylan had lied by omission about confronting Del Howe and had been running a secret investigation behind her back to track the New Castle Killer's movements. He'd used his position as a deputy—used her—as a means to an end. Not illegally, but the hurt from that choice almost outweighed the good he'd done. She'd trained herself to endure emotional loneliness since losing her family, but for the first time in twenty years, someone had helped her feel more than the numbness she'd accepted as her future. He'd helped her.

Remi forced herself to look past the pain, past the lies, past the intense need to separate herself from him, and considered the man. Not the private investigator who hadn't given up on the four-year-old boy who'd gone missing. Not the marshal who'd backed up her and her team on countless assignments over the past six months. But the man she'd slowly fallen in love with over the course of this investigation.

The man she knew. The one who'd followed her to the safe house when he'd learned she was a possible target of a killer. The one who'd made mouth-watering mac and cheese that'd magically taken the emptiness inside her away. The one who'd held her under the shower when she couldn't stand on her own. That man would never resort to inflicting the kind of pain he despised on another human being.

She swallowed around the dryness in her throat

as the road ahead of her came into focus. "Yes, I believe him, and I'll believe and stand up for any one of the marshals in my division who finds themselves in a similar situation."

"Then that's good enough for me," Foster said. "Reed, Watson and I are headed your way now."

The call ended, throwing her into an unsettling silence between her own thoughts and the hum of the tires against cement. The GPS on her phone pinged, signaling she was almost to Annabell Ross's home, but she had to assume the woman herself had become another victim of the madman behind this game. Annabell would've been a loose end, a witness, and the killer would've gone out of his way to ensure she never talked. Remi only hoped she made it in time to keep Dylan from meeting a similar end. "Just be alive."

She pulled into the small, quiet neighborhood, and slammed on the brakes. The small blue house and bright yellow door did nothing to ease the racing panic threatening to tear her apart from the inside. Grabbing Dylan's weapon and badge from the console, she hit the pavement and rounded the bumper of the SUV. Hauling the cargo door open, she quickly strapped into her Kevlar. She shoved his duty weapon down the back of her cargo pants before clipping his badge to her vest. Didn't matter Dylan wasn't a US marshal in her division anymore. She wasn't going to lose him. Not again.

The pounding of her boots against the driveway bounced off the overhang above the garage door as she sprinted for the front door. Testing the handle, Remi backed off a few feet. Locked. She shifted her weight onto her back leg and slammed her heel into the space beside the dead bolt. Wood splintered under the pressure, and the door swung back into the wall behind it. Weapon up, finger beside the trigger, she breached. "US Marshals! Is anybody here?"

No answer.

She swung her attention to her left, clearing the living room as she crossed the small entryway toward the dining room and kitchen behind three large archways carved into the wall.

A wall of odor slammed into her. She stepped under the main arch into the kitchen. Nothing looked disturbed or out of place, but she couldn't ignore the sickeningly-sweet smell of death in the air. Remi stepped into thc hallway, fighting the urge to cover her mouth and nose with her hands. She couldn't afford to compromise her position. No matter the situation.

Her boots dragged against old carpeting that silenced her approach toward the back bedroom where the odor seemed to originate. Ignoring her reflection in the mirror in the bathroom to her left, she nudged the door open. Empty. Same for the second bedroom, which contained nothing more than a single twin-size bed.

Dylan had called her less than twenty minutes ago. Even if he'd been killed, he woudn't have decomposed this quickly. Remi braced herself for the worst as she pushed open the door.

Annabell Ross stared back at her. Nausea churned in Remi's gut as she took in signs of strangulation. Dylan had been right. The hiker who'd left traces of volcanic rock in his footprints outside Del Howe's cabin had been their killer all along. He'd used Annabell as an alibi then killed her when she wasn't of any use.

The faces of the New Castle Killer's victims had been engrained into her head, over and over. She would've recognized him at the scene. She was sure of it. Remi lowered her weapon. But now that she thought about it, the male witness had put his back to her when she'd left the cabin with Captain Paulson and Sergeant Nguyen. She hadn't thought much of it at the time the hiker had been giving his statement, but it's possible he'd avoided facing her on purpose.

She took a single step forward, and the crunch of metal and glass tore her gaze from the young woman sprawled across the bed. Thickness coated the edges of her throat as she realized what she'd stepped on. A phone.

Heavy footsteps echoed down the hall from the main living space. “Chief, you in here?”

Watson’s voice penetrated the ringing in her ears. She crouched down and collected Dylan’s phone. He’d been here. Backup had arrived, and now she had to find him. “Back here! Inform Gresham PD we need a crime scene unit.”

Three deputies crowded into the room one at a time. Finnick Reed, Jonah Watson and Beckett Foster all covered their noses and mouths in one move. Her team.

“Where’s Cove?” Foster asked.

A deep-throated scream answered in response.

BLOOD TRICKLED DOWN his inner thigh as his attacker retracted the blade.

Dylan struggled against the ropes keeping him tied to the chair and pressed his toes into the ground. The muscles in his jaw ached from the pressure of holding in his screams. In vain. Four lacerations, all of varying lengths and depths. Just as the New Castle Killer had done to his victims. Sweat built on his upper lip as the pain receded, and he dropped his head back.

“Don’t give up on me now, Cove. We still have so much to talk about.” A lean, muscular frame escaped from the shadows cast by the trees surrounding them from every side. Tad Marrow, the New Castle Killer’s third and last victim, stepped into the beam of moonlight coming through the trees. Miles of forest expanded in each direction, ensuring no matter where Dylan ran, he couldn't escape.

At six-three, Marrow carried himself well for a dead man. Dark green eyes, almost black, cut through his pain. Sharp cheekbones, thin lips and a prominent widow's peak aged the man Dylan knew to be in his early twenties. Dozens of white, puckered lines of scar tissue interrupted the skin along his face, neck and hands. He switched off the blade between both hands then set the tip against Dylan's cheek. "I came to you for help. I believed you when you said you'd look into my case as soon as you could. I waited weeks for you to contact me, but your call never came."

The blade dropped down and sliced into his arm. This time deeper. Dylan bit back the growl clawing up his throat. That was what his attacker wanted, to know he was causing the same pain as the New Castle Killer had caused him. But Dylan wasn't going to play along.

Tad Marrow had killed twenty-seven people, including the killer who'd abducted him. The former veterinarian's assistant had started his career with helping the sick and afflicted, but now he was nothing more than a serial killer who fed off his victims' agony.

"You're right, Tad, and I'm sorry. I should've

connected the dots sooner. I should've been there for you instead of believing your case had nothing to do with Del Howe, but killing me isn't going to make that pain go away," he said.

"I don't need your apology, Cove. It's too late for that. What I need is for you to know what it feels like to lose every last bit of hope you've ever had. I need you to know that when I'm through with you, I'm going to find Remington Barton. I'm going to make her scream, and there will be nothing you can do about it." Tad pressed the blade's edge against Dylan's inner arm. "But don't worry, you'll still be alive for that part. You'd be surprised how much pain and blood loss the human body can take."

"You won't have the chance." He braced against the oncoming pain, pulling at the length of rope around his wrists and ankles. He held his breath as Marrow swept the blade over his skin. He wrenched from side to side to escape.

Tad Marrow took a step back, his face half hidden in shadow, and fanned his hands out in front of him. "I never lost count, you know. I could still tell you the exact order Howe cut into me. I'd always believed the brain automatically blocked that kind of trauma to keep from having to experience it over and over, but I remember everything. Every detail, every scream."

Dylan tried to breathe through the remnants of

fire burning up his arm. His shirt stuck to his skin, the waistband of his jeans soaked with blood. His heart rate spiked into dangerous territory. He had to get some control. The more he panicked, the faster he'd bleed out. He needed to keep Marrow distracted, give Remi and the team enough time to find him. Because she was coming. He had to believe that. He had to believe what they'd had these past few days was more important than the lies he'd told her and himself. "You escaped, Tad. You could've started over, could've gotten help. Instead, you went out of your way to kill every investigator, dispatcher and emergency tech who'd been involved in the New Castle case."

"They failed us!" Marrow struck out with the knife and another gut-wrenching shot of pain ripped through Dylan's leg. "You connected Del Howe to the New Castle Killer case, but do you even know how long he kept us? How long he tortured us? Do you know we were drugged and kept in a cargo van with tinted windows so we could see people passing us on the street? Close enough to help, but too far away to hear us scream."

Dylan hadn't known any of that. He worked his wrists inside the rope, focusing on the sting of his other wounds to detract from the awareness of the strands cutting into him. "No. I don't know, and I understand why you might not have wanted to come forward to testify. There were no guarantees

Del Howe wouldn't come for you again or come for a family member to hurt you more. You escaped your captor, but you're still a prisoner. Killing me—killing Remi—won't change that, Tad. I can help you. I made a mistake not listening to you in Delaware, but what you're doing only ends with more blood on your hands. Let me help you now."

"Help me? I don't need your help, Cove." Marrow circled behind the chair, out of sight. The sound of snapping twigs and fallen leaves under his attacker's feet faded. Strong hands dug into Dylan's shoulders, arching his back away from the chair. "No. You see, I'm grateful for what happened in Delaware. If Howe hadn't tried to make me a victim, I never would've become the predator. I'm not the man you knew, Cove. I'm stronger, smarter, and for the first time in my life, I have answers to why I was chosen. He gave me purpose, you see, a reason to keep going. Soon, you'll learn you can only rely on yourself. It took me a bit longer while I was under the knife, close to three hundred cuts, before I realized no one was coming to save me." Marrow whispered in Dylan's ear. "I'm interested to hear when that happens for you."

The seventh cut sliced alongside the top of Dylan's spine, and another scream escaped. Pain hit his brain in endless waves. He jerked against the ropes as hard as he could, and the shift in weight lifted two chair legs out of the mud. He tipped to his right and hit the ground hard, his head snapping back. Air rushed from his lungs. Sweat beaded along his forehead and slid into his hairline. No. This wasn't how he was going to die. "You killed Del Howe to show you were better than him?"

"The New Castle Killer was weak." Rounding in front of him, Marrow crouched, the blade between his hands. "The day I escaped that van, I'd somehow lived through another day of bloodletting. I couldn't swallow, couldn't even seem to blink. While Howe was cleaning the blood off the floor, I managed to get one hand free from the rope. He had his back to me, convinced I wasn't a threat. He never heard me untie the other ropes, never saw me coming. I grabbed this knife—" Marrow set the tip of the blade against his finger and seesawed the handle side to side "—and I thrust it into his back. I could tell he was just waiting for me to finish the job, but at the time, all I could think about was escape. Even at my lowest, I was stronger than he was, and I showed him that. Although, I can't deny how good it felt to make him suffer as I had, to hear him scream."

"You used Sergeant Nguyen's identity and police resources to track Del Howe." The pieces were starting to fall into place. "You registered for law enforcement conferences in his name so you could hunt and kill anyone involved in the original case in those cities. But what about Annabell Ross? She didn't have anything to do with the New Castle Killer case. She was a hiker who loved the outdoors. You used her for her knowledge of nearby caves, and as an alibi that day at the scene, then strangled her when you didn't need her anymore." Dylan worked his hand back and forth, back and forth, to gain some slack in the rope. "She was innocent."

"Every master needs a set of tools to complete his work, Cove." Marrow tipped the blade straight up in the air between them. "You should know that better than anyone considering you used Remington Barton and her position with the marshals for your own investigation."

"We're nothing alike." Rage coiled hot and fast in Dylan's gut. He stretched his right hand away from the chair to feel the earth around him. He had to find something—anything—strong enough to cut through the ropes or to be used as a weapon.

Marrow had ambushed him in Annabell Ross's house. He wouldn't let the perp get the upper hand again. Not when he was the only one standing between Remi and the SOB in front of him. The tip of his middle finger hit the edge of something rough and solid. A rock. He pushed back the pain in his shoulders as he contracted the muscles in his spine and stretched even farther. The stitches in his side screamed as he pressed the raw edge of rock into his palms.

"I can see why the sheriff likes you. I bet that aggressive streak you show off is what drew her in back in Delaware. But it wasn't enough, was it?" Marrow's low, menacing laugh cut through him. "She figured out who you really are, and now you're more like me than you think. Unbalanced, defective. Alone. Don't worry, once I'm finished, she won't live long enough to hold it against you."

"Go to hell." Dylan used the rock to cut through the rope around his wrists. Straightening his legs, he slid the cables at his ankles over the ends of the chair. He shot forward, colliding with his attacker, and wrapped his grip around the blade's handle before Marrow could take his next breath. They hit the ground as one and struggled for control of the weapon.

Only, Dylan wasn't fast enough. The knife pierced through skin and muscle and collided into bone. Voices echoed from the trees, and Marrow placed a strong hand over his mouth, stifling his call for help.

"Looks like we have company, Cove." Marrow withdrew the blade from Dylan's gut, straightened and wiped the steel on his pant leg. He stepped over his prey, but Dylan couldn't force his hands to reach out to stop him. "Don't worry, I'll be the perfect host."

Chapter Fourteen

"Fan out. Foster, you're with me. Reed and Watson, head north." Remi faced the tree line, weapon in hand, and hit the power button on her tactical flashlight. Four beams pooled on the ground as the remaining three members of her team split off from her side and disappeared into the shadows. Dylan was out here. Alone, in pain. His scream echoed through her head as she headed into the woods. Her heels sank into the damp grass as she crossed Annabell Ross's backyard. She pinched the push-to-talk button on the radio strapped to her Kevlar, the atmospheric scent of rain thick in the air. "Comms check."

"Watson." The deputy's light gave away his position off to her right and a few meters ahead. "Nothing yet."

"I've got something that looks like drag marks here. Approximately twenty meters north of your position, Chief." Static interrupted the constant pattering of rain against her shoulders as the signal broke up. "This is Reed, by the way."

"Damn it, Reed, we know it's you." Deputy Beckett Foster's outline slowed to her left. Of the five members of the team, she trusted his experience hunting fugitives over her own instincts to race through the woods, blind and half cocked, until she found Cove. "Watson, you and Reed follow those tracks. Could be our guy or an animal."

"Report back if your situation changes." Hair clung to her face as Remi craned her mouth toward the radio. "Our suspect has now killed twenty-seven people we know of, guys. Stay alert. Watch each other's backs. Cove is one of ours. I want to keep it that way."

She wanted to keep him for herself.

"We'll bring him home, Chief," Watson said.

Remi forced one foot in front of the other, mud suctioning her boots into the earth. Visibility dropped the farther they left Annabell's home behind. Their suspect preferred to work in the dark. At some point over the past few years, he'd become part of it, but she wouldn't lose Dylan to the shadows. The muscles around her stab wound ached the longer she held her weapon shoulder-height, but she wasn't going to be caught by surprise this time. "Where are you, Dylan?"

"Chief, you're…want…this." Reed. Damn it. Their signal was losing strength. "Chief…hear…me?"

Her skin chilled as she scoured the trees ahead for a sign of Reed's and Watson's flashlights, but pitch blackness had consumed their position. Glancing over her shoulder, she caught sight of Foster a few yards to her left. She pinched the radio in her grip. "Reed, say again."

"Signal's weak," Foster said. "A few more meters and the radios are going to be useless. We have to keep going. Maybe the closer we get to their position, the better we'll be able to stay in contact."

"Chief!" A gunshot exploded from nearby, drowning Watson's voice over the radio, and every cell in Remi's body caught fire.

She darted in the direction she'd last seen Reed and Watson, her heart in her throat. Foster followed close on her heels. Branches reached out and caught the skin along her neck and face, and tangled with her hair, but she wouldn't stop. Not until she knew every member of her team was alive. Sweat built between her palm and her weapon, and she tightened her grip. Mud, fallen branches and patches of leaves fought to trip her up. Slowing, she glanced back to calculate how far she'd run. She battled to steady her breathing. Running a hand through her hair to get it out of her face, Remi spun. No sign of Reed or Watson. No other flashlights. No movement. "They were right here."

"Chief." Foster kicked through a pile of foliage. A beam of light spread across the dirt and highlighted the marshal's black boots. It arched up the base of a large pine beside him, reflecting off something embedded in the bark.

"One flashlight. Where is the second?" She bent to examine the metal stuck in the tree. She secured her weapon and pulled her pocketknife from her ankle holster. She pried the metal loose, and it fell into her palm. "It's a slug. 9mm."

"One of ours." Foster studied the surrounding trees. "Reed or Watson got a shot off, but not before they were taken out. He's out here, picking us off one by one."

"He's comfortable in the dark. He uses it against his victims and feeds off their terror of being alone. I wouldn't be surprised if he scouted the area before tonight to memorize the landscape." She cut off the shiver working up her spine as memories from the caves escaped the box at the back of her mind. They'd faced killers as a team. Amateurs, apprentices, veteran serial killers. None of them compared to the monster hunting them now. Remi pocketed the expended slug and holstered her knife. Drawing her sidearm, she hit the power for her flashlight.

They couldn't win this. Not directly. To catch a killer, she had to start thinking like one. She had to use the predator's strengths against him. "Turn off your light. Rely on your hearing, and keep your movements to a minimum. Our priority is recovering our team, but if you find the suspect at the end of your weapon, you sure as hell better take him down. Understand?"

"Yes, ma'am." Foster killed his flashlight, his outline blending into the shadows closing in around them.

"Good." They moved as one, slowly at first, as their vision adjusted to the lack of light. Buzzing insects quieted the deeper they treaded through the woods. Her own shallow breaths filled her ears, but she felt more than saw Foster to her left. An owl made its presence known somewhere overhead as low bushes and leaves swayed with the wind. The rain had stopped, but puddles of water still sloshed under her boots.

"I know you're out here, Sheriff," a deep, overly familiar voice said. "I've already taken care of three members of your team. You wouldn't leave them to die as you left me to face Del Howe alone, would you?"

Remi stopped. Reed, Watson, Cove. The killer hadn't only come for her and Dylan, he'd attacked her team. Holding her breath, she searched the trees for the source of the voice, for something to give away the killer's position. Movement registered to her left, and she realized Foster was working his way toward the voice. With any luck, they could cut the killer off before he even realized what was happening. No. She wasn't going anywhere.

"You weren't able to protect the officers involved in the New Castle Killer case, Sheriff." The voice had somehow changed position without warning, just as it had in the lava tubes. "What makes you think you could protect anyone else?"

He was right. How could she protect her team when she didn't know who the hell she was protecting them from?

A struggle reached her ears from where Foster had been standing a few seconds before, and Remi raised her weapon. She clicked on her flashlight and scanned a few feet out, giving away her position. He'd vanished. Leaves bounced as though they'd been disturbed, but he wasn't there. "Foster!"

No answer.

Damn it. Her weapon shook with the tremors working through her hands. Was he still alive? Were the others? She killed the light and ducked behind the cover of a large bush to her right. Crouching, she aimed her weapon down between her knees and settled back against a tree large enough to conceal her size. She pressed the crown of her head into the bark, focusing on the sting of pain instead of the doubt clawing up her throat. She'd spent her entire life fighting to survive. First, after losing her family and growing up on the streets of her hometown. Second, to prove her gender had nothing to do with her ability to run a USMS division. But this…this was different. This was her team, the men she'd come to trust, to care about. The men who believed in her.

"It's just you and me, Remington. Cove is bleeding out where I left him, and the rest of your team is out of the equation." A twig snapped a few feet in front of her before a large, muscular outline materialized. He kept moving diagonally away from her, unaware his prey was so close. "You and I both know one of us is going down. Time to end this, don't you think?"

Cove. Rage burned under her skin, growing hotter and more out of control. The muscles in her jaw ached as she clamped her back teeth and balanced her weight into her heels. Straightening, she stepped into the open. The killer had made a mistake this time. He'd gone after the only man who'd made her feel as though she was enough, who'd broken past her emotional defenses and released a stronger part of herself she'd never known existed.

Keeping her steps light, Remi closed the distance between her and the killer who'd nearly murdered everyone involved in the New Castle Killer case. Only this time, she was ready. They'd met him on his own turf, but she'd make damn sure she and her team were the ones who walked away.

He didn't think she was a threat. She'd prove him wrong. "You know, for once I agree with you."

The killer spun around, and she swung her weapon as hard as she could. The butt of her gun slammed into his head, and he collapsed at her feet.

"It is time to end this." She took aim.

Recovering faster than she thought possible, her abductor wrapped his hand around her arm and pulled her hard toward the ground. Standing, he twisted her elbow until pain ignited through her nervous system. He forced her to drop her weapon. "But are you going to save your team or save yourself?"

DYLAN SLAMMED HIS fist into the ground, using every last ounce of strength to pull himself up out of the dirt.

Remi had come for him. Her voice hadn't been a hallucination, but she wasn't alone. Reed, Foster, Watson. They were out here, too. They were all in danger. A pain-filled growl escaped his chest as he pressed himself into a sitting position. He had to get up. He had to get to her before Tad Marrow did.

Blood slicked the inside of his arms and waistband. A thud broke through the constant buzz of crickets and other wildlife he couldn't see. Dylan put everything he had left into getting to his feet, his left leg dragging slightly behind. He secured a hand over the shallow stab wound in his side. Agony tore the air from his lungs, and he stumbled forward. He doubled over, reaching for the nearest tree for balance. He was bleeding, but he wasn't going to let Marrow take Remi from him. He'd already lost her when she'd discovered his motives for joining USMS. He wasn't going to fail her again.

The echo of punches landing filled his ears, and he forced himself to slow his pulse to listen to the source. There, to the left, about twenty feet. His senses had adjusted, only a few streaks of moonlight highlighting Remi's smaller build. Adrenaline dumped into his veins. Dylan picked up the pace, the pain disappearing to the back of his mind, as he charged through the underbrush toward her. "Remi!"

He collided with the killer dragging Remi closer. Trees, shadows, the ground—it all became one in his vision as he hit the dirt. They rolled, each fighting for dominance, down an incline before slamming into the base of a tree. Scrambling to his feet, Dylan struck the bastard as hard as he could. A kick landed dead center below his sternum and knocked him off balance. He stumbled back as Remi moved in. Warning shot through him as Marrow elbowed her straight into the kidney, and while a sharp gasp reached Dylan's ears, she didn't let it slow her down.

She positioned her calf behind her attacker's opposite leg and shoved him forward. Remi and Marrow flipped through the air a split second before he rocketed his fist into her face. She collapsed to one side, and Dylan moved in.

Cocking his elbow back, he landed a solid hit to Marrow's jaw, but in the next moment had his feet kicked straight out from under him. Clouds billowed above as heavier rain pitted the soil. Marrow stood over him, rage tightening his body language. Moonlight reflected off metal. "You failed me when I needed you the most, Cove. I'm going to save the next victim the trouble of trusting you."

A frustrated scream was all the warning he heard as Remi clawed to her feet and ran straight for Marrow. She wrapped her grip around the SOB's wrist, twisted under his front side and hauled him completely over her back.

Marrow slammed into the ground, a groan breaching the heavy pounding of Dylan's heartbeat.

Remi removed another weapon she'd stashed at her low back, but Marrow swiped a blade across her midsection before she got off a shot. She maneuvered out of the way, and her weapon discharged, the bullet whizzing past Cove's ear.

Marrow raised his knife high above his head and brought it down, aiming for her heart.

Remi dropped the gun and caught his wrist mere centimeters from her chest, giving Dylan leverage while Marrow was distracted. He thrust his fist into the killer's gut. Marrow hauled his heel into Remi's stomach, and she fell back.

Turning to Dylan, Marrow circled left. Dylan brought up his arms to block the oncoming hit. Marrow jabbed from the right, bounded behind him and aimed the knife at Dylan's neck. Strain built in the muscles along Dylan's forearms and chest as the tip of the blade drew closer. Wedged between Marrow and an excruciating death, his entire body screamed for relief.

Out of the corner of his eye, Remi struggled to her feet, and within seconds Marrow was using Dylan as a shield.

"Killing Cove isn't going to make up for the past, Tad. If he could go back and change what happened, I'm sure he would." She'd recognized the killer. Beams of soft moonlight passed through the trees and highlighted her every move. She peeled the Velcro straps away at her sides and tossed her Kevlar to the ground. "But everything that happened in Delaware? That was because of me. You said it yourself—one of us is going down." Blood-tinged rain rolled down her face in uneven lines. She shifted her weight between both feet and raised her fists. "Let him go. I'm the one you really want."

She was baiting a serial killer, putting herself at risk in an attempt to save one of her deputies. Former deputies. Dylan struggled to keep the blade from penetrating his artery as Marrow increased the pressure.

"What's to stop me from getting everything I want?" Marrow asked.

"Because there are five of us and one of you." The muscle in Remi's jaw ticked, and Dylan recognized the lie for what it was. There was no backup. No one else coming to save them. She was giving Dylan a chance to escape.

"I like those odds." Marrow released his hold and Dylan ducked out from his reach.

The killer lunged forward, knife in hand.

Remi pulled a small knife from her ankle a split second before Marrow struck.

"No!" Dylan lunged.

Catching Marrow around the waist, he held tight. An elbow connected with the hypersensitive nerves around his temple and snapped his head back. Wrenching Marrow over his midsection, Dylan propelled the three of them down a steep incline.

In his next breath, cold water consumed all of them from head to toe. He lost his footing then kicked hard to get his head above water. Fisting Tad Marrow's shirt with one hand to keep from being dragged under the surface, he rocketed his fist into the killer's head. "Get your damn hands off of her."

Marrow fell back into the inky wet darkness, pulling Remi with him into the depths.

Her scream cut off as she disappeared right in front of Dylan.

Bubbles tickled along his face and neck as he dove. Weeds and algae clung to him as Marrow pushed Remi toward the bottom of the lake.

He stretched to reach the killer, trying to wrench Marrow away from her, but the water slowed him down. Pressure built in his lungs. Remi and Marrow spun in circles, each trying to get the upper hand until Marrow's blade carved through the water. Toward Remi.

Dylan gripped both hands around Marrow's arm and pulled him back. Time distorted into a cold fluid as Dylan wrapped his arms and legs around Marrow in an attempt to weigh him down. His heart threatened to beat straight out of his chest as dark outlines appeared above the surface. Stained water blossomed around him, and he realized he was still bleeding from the stab wound he'd sustained. Didn't matter. He just had to hold on, had to give Remi a chance. He'd promised to keep her safe, and he'd do whatever it took to keep his word. For her. He pulled them toward the bottom of the lake, and his lower back finally hit silt and sand.

Marrow's attempt to free himself became sluggish. A series of jerks coursed through the killer's body, but Dylan still wouldn't let go. The man had somehow escaped death, killed twenty-seven people and attempted to kill two others, including Remi. He wasn't going anywhere.

Several flashlight beams filtered down from the surface, and then she was there. Right in front of him. Long black hair floated around her beautiful face. Remi slid her hands over his. Her eyes settled on him, and the pressure in his lungs and the pain in his side disappeared. There was only Remi.

She smoothed her thumb across the back of his hand, silently pleading for him to let go. But Marrow had beaten death once. There were no guarantees he'd spend the rest of his life behind bars for what he'd done or if the DA could tie him to the other murders all across the country. Every second the bastard lived, Remi's life would be at stake. Tad Marrow would never stop coming for her.

Remi set her fingers over Dylan's mouth and shook her head. Bubbles sped toward the surface as Marrow went still his grip. Fisting her hands in his shirt, she closed the distance between them and turned his head toward her. Her lips met his, and the past two years, the New Castle Killer investigation, the scene at Del Howe's cabin—it all faded until one moment remained. He and Remi sitting at the kitchen table eating the peanut butter, jelly and chip sandwiches, her smile brighter and more freeing than anything he'd ever experienced. He'd known then. He'd known, no matter what happened between them or if she'd discovered the truth, he wouldn't be able to let her go. Not again. She'd become more than his chief over these past six months.

She was everything.

Dylan released Marrow, his arms and legs heavy. His chief shoved the killer toward the surface. Kicking off the bottom of the lake, Dylan followed, and the pain returned. Blood stained the water around him as hints of sunrise broke through the surrounding woods. Reality sped up as he crashed through the surface and clawed his way toward shore. He collapsed onto his back, staring up at the last remnants of storm clouds.

Reed dragged the killer's unconscious form from the water and started counting off chest compressions. Watson breathed into his mouth, and within a minute, Marrow choked up fistfuls of water. Foster turned the man onto his side, his expression guarded as he pulled a set of cuffs from his lower back.

And Remi… She stood over them all, every bit the woman and deputy chief who'd gone out of her way to protect her team. She wiped a trail of blood from her mouth before helping Reed roll the killer to his stomach. "Tad Marrow, you are under arrest."

Chapter Fifteen

"Madison has been able to tie thirteen of the twenty-seven murders to Tad Marrow." Watson handed Remi a manila file folder, the contents of which laid out the FBI's case against the only victim who'd ever escaped the New Castle Killer. Once they'd been able to prove Tad Marrow had crossed state lines, the Bureau had taken full jurisdiction. "She's still working through the rest. The baby might be trying to destroy us through sleep deprivation, but she's got a good set of deputy district attorney's taking on some of the work."

Remi set the folder across her lap, careful not to let the crime scene photos slide from the hospital bed. Stinging pain spread through her side. Torn stitches, recovering concussion, additional bruises and lacerations.

She sifted through the evidence log pulled together from the FBI's detailed search of Annabell Ross's home which Marrow had used as a stronghold after killing the woman. Rope matching the strands used in half a dozen of the murders, including the marks left behind on Annabell Ross, Dylan and Remi's own wrists. A sheath for the blade recovered from the bottom of the lake following the fight in the woods with DNA embedded in the leather. Fingerprints. The documents Sergeant Nguyen had reported stolen after the break in two years prior with a driver's license using Marrow's photo. The credit card used to book reservations in six of the cities where several of her former colleagues had been murdered. It was all there, and it would be enough to put the bastard away for the rest of his life. "Is Marrow saying anything about the deaths Madison hasn't been able to tie to him?"

"Not yet, but I'm sure she and her team are working on some kind of deal that might loosen his tongue." Watson sat back in his chair beside the bed, his gaze more intense than a few minutes before. "But that's not what you wanted to ask me about, was it?"

She flipped the file closed and set it on the table to left, heat climbing from her chest into her neck and face. No. That hadn't been the question she'd wanted to ask, but she was still the chief deputy of the Oregon division and Watson's superior officer, for the time being. Personal questions clouded that relationship. "I might have been injured in the line of duty, Deputy Watson, but I can still make sure you never walk again for prying."

"My lawyer might have a problem with that," he said.

"The district attorney is not your personal lawyer." She swallowed a laugh threatening to pop her new set of stitches.

"I'm pretty sure it became part of the deal when we had a kid together." Watson's smile drained from his expression. The former FBI bomb technician had been trained to spot the details, to make sure nothing had slipped his attention during an investigation. It was one of the things that'd initially impressed her when he'd applied for the marshals, but Remi suddenly felt as though she'd become the next puzzle for him to solve. "Reed informed me Cove is out of surgery. He and Foster are standing guard outside his room. He's awake and talking."

"That's good." She couldn't deny the flood of relief coursing through her, and neither could Watson, she was sure. Lowering her gaze to an invisible thread in the hospital bedsheet, Remi forced herself to breathe evenly through the pain suctioning to the black hole in her chest. "You know, I hired Cove to work the New Castle Killer case in Delaware. He was the best investigator I'd worked with, including some of the men and women in my own department. He's always had this...responsibility inside him. Like it was up to him to solve every case he took on, and I admired that."

Watson didn't answer.

"But now..." Remi cleared her throat. "I suspended Cove after Gresham PD searched his apartment. They uncovered evidence he was using USMS resources to fund his own investigation into the New Castle Killer, and the forensic report from the cabin placed him at the scene before Del Howe was murdered."

She stared at the bag of her belongings resting on the bench below the single window to her right. Her boots, clothing, two badges side by side. Hers and Dylan's. She'd had both in her possession when she'd confronted Tad Marrow, but now the space between those two chunks of metal seemed impossibly wide.

"To be honest, Watson, I wasn't surprised. His determination to uncover the truth was why I'd manipulated the system to get him into this division in the first place. I wanted him to apply the same methods he'd taken on in Delaware to our cases here, but then I found out he lied. That he used my position as chief deputy to catch a killer. So I took his badge and his weapon and everything they represented away from him. I made it personal so I could hurt him as much as he'd hurt me." She shook her head as though the simple motion could rewind time. "I left Delaware and the

New Castle Killer case—I left him—behind to take back some tiny part of control in my life after I was forced out as sheriff, but now that the case is solved, I feel more out of control than ever. How is that possible?"

"Love is like that. It has a funny way of making us feel in control and lost at the same time. Anchored and desperate. Strong and exposed." Watson leaned forward, resting his elbows on his knees. "I've watched the way your eyes get lighter when he's around, Chief. I've seen how hard it is for him not to touch you while we're on assignment. I'm not sure you even notice, but the rest of us have, and me, Foster, Reed—we all had to learn the same lesson when we fell for the women we were meant to love."

"What lesson?" The words slipped past her lips without permission.

"Loving someone completely isn't about control." The marshal stood, turning toward the door. Setting one hand on the handle, he faced her. "It's about trusting them with your weaknesses—your mistakes—and having the guts to accept what comes next."

Watson wrenched open the door and disappeared into the hallway.

Love wasn't about control. The words echoed in her head as Remi pulled back the sheets and set her bare feet on the cold tile. She peeled off the blood pressure cuff from around her arm, the Velcro too loud in her ears, and ripped the sticky monitors from her skin. Leaving the mess of tubes and wires in the bed, she went to the window. Watson had been right. She'd spent every day of her life since the fire determined to prove that emotions, weaknesses and mistakes hadn't affected her climb out of the past, and she'd paid the physical, mental and emotion price in return.

Her family was gone because she hadn't been strong enough to pull them from the fire. The New Castle Killer had escaped because she hadn't been intelligent enough to stay ahead of him. A serial killer had nearly murdered her entire investigative team because she hadn't been brave enough to face her mistakes.

But Dylan had made her feel like…she was enough.

She'd tried to keep him at an emotionally safe distance, but the truth was she needed him. More than she'd ever needed anyone in her life. To surprise her with mac and cheese, to take away the nightmares, to force her to break through the numbness and unshoulder the weight she'd carried all these years. He'd witnessed her weaknesses and embraced them for what they were: part of her. And despite her parting words when she'd suspended him, she trusted him.

Remi discarded the gown and dressed. After

collecting both badges from the bench beneath the window, she ignored the slight dampness of her pants and boots and left the room.

Dylan had taken on one of the most dangerous killers in the history of the country to protect her. She wasn't sure she could ever repay him, but he deserved to know about the good he'd done for Del Howe's and Tad Marrow's victims. The families would have justice. They'd have closure. They could move on with their lives, and it was time for her to do the same.

Reed turned from his position beside what she assumed to be Dylan's hospital room door as she approached. A deep laceration across his brow had been stitched—most likely with Reed's own two hands—but a few drops of blood remained on the collar of his superhero T-shirt peeking out from beneath his Kevlar vest. "Looking good, Chief. All the blood is gone."

"Can't say the same for you." She pointed to the stains as she stopped in front of the door.

"Camille is bringing me a new one as soon as she finishes up photographing the scene for the bureau." Chiseled cheekbones and boyish blue eyes radiated pure adoration at the mention of his witness-turned-fiancée. "Seems they were so impressed with her work tracking down and photographing what was left of The Carver's victims, they want her to join their team full-time for this case. She'll get to travel again and use her photography for something good. Just like she wanted."

"I don't blame them for wanting to keep her on. She's an impressive woman." To have a passion destroyed by a serial killer's obsession to becoming one of the most sought after serial crime scene photographers in the county took guts, and Remi couldn't help but admire Reed's support and admiration for the woman he loved.

She set her hand on the door leading into Dylan's room. Dylan had used her and the USMS to solve the New Castle Killer case, but he'd never questioned her innocence in Del Howe's death. He'd followed her every lead, believed in her, supported her. Whether he'd done it to advance his own investigation, she didn't know, but there was only one way to find out. "Well, whatever you two need—days off to travel with her, transferring to a new district if they want her in DC—let me know."

"I'm not going anywhere, Chief," Reed said. "None of us are. We're a team. You, me, Foster, Watson and Cove. Where you go, we go. Besides, who are you going to have to save when we're all getting picked off by a psychotic killer looking for revenge if we're gone?"

"I'm glad you're okay, Reed. Even if I wish you had an off button I could hit sometimes." She caught sight of Beckett Foster headed down the hall, two coffees in hand.

The fugitive recovery expert nodded, handing one cup off to Reed before he offered her the second. Circles had deepened under his eyes. Another case of sleep deprivation brought on by a tiny human. "Figured I find you here instead of obeying your doctor's orders to take it easy. Coffee, black."

"Thanks. For everything." The warmth penetrated through her foam cup and into her palms, but it wasn't anywhere close to the heat she craved from the man on the other side of the door. She had her team's backs, and they had hers, but right then Remi wanted more. "We wouldn't have been able to take down Tad Marrow without either of you, but now, if you don't mind, I'm far more interested in the deputy on the other side of this door than either of you."

She pushed into Dylan's room.

"GOING SOMEWHERE?" THAT VOICE. Her voice. It penetrated through him, more determined than ever to reach past the pain and soothe the rough edges left behind by their last conversation.

The muscles down his spine constricted one by one. Dylan hiked his jeans around his waist, careful of the new set of stitches and gauze in his side. Jagged shards of pain sliced into muscle and stole the air from his lungs. He leveraged his weight into his hand against the end of the bed frame. Facing her, he maneuvered back onto the edge of the mattress and raised his gaze to hers for the first time since she'd taken his badge. The world tore through him in an instant, hours speeding up and combining into mere seconds. Muffled orders and flashes of light infiltrated the shadows then narrowed to a mere brush of her voice.

Remi had been in those woods.

She'd come for him despite the fact the evidence had revealed he'd used her and the marshals for his own agenda. She'd put herself between him and Tad Marrow to save his life. "That was the plan. Figured I'd be able to make it down the hall, but I've got to tell you, putting on pants has never been so damn difficult."

"It took me three tries to tie my boots." Iridescent blue eyes lowered to the floor as one corner of her gorgeous mouth pulled into a half smile. "Seems surviving a knife wound isn't all it's cracked up to be."

He laughed and pressed both hands into the top of his knees in an attempt to stay upright, but the room was already spinning. Not from any injury. Although, he'd lost an excessive amount of blood. Because of her. "What are you doing here, Sheriff?"

"I wanted to let you know the DA has been able to connect about half of the murders Watson uncovered during the investigation to Tad Marrow so far. She's still working on the others, but the FBI has plenty of physical evidence to prove he's the one who killed Del Howe in that cabin. They recovered rope matching the strands used to bind the victim, and the blade dredged from the bottom of the lake matches the lacerations inflicted before death. With all that, Gresham PD has closed their case against you, and they've cut me loose as a suspect."

She shrugged. "We'll still be required to testify at Marrow's trial, but you, for all intents and purposes, are a free man." She slid her hands into her cargo pant pockets, stains of dirt and blood crusted against the dark green fabric. "The bullet they pulled from your side matches a weapon Sergeant Nguyen reported stolen during the break-in at his home two years ago, too. Because of you, Tad Marrow is going away for a very long time. Thought I should be the one to tell you, considering I'm the one who got you into this mess in the first place."

"I appreciate it." He didn't know what else to say. Maybe there was nothing else for him to say. He'd known exactly what had been at risk when he'd joined the marshals to hunt the New Castle Killer. He'd known using her and USMS resources would sever any friendship they'd built over the past three years. What he hadn't expected was for the disappointment—the betrayal—in her gaze to tear him apart.

Dylan slowly got to his feet, every stitch in his side stretching into discomfort, but he couldn't stand the distance between them anymore. Not after what they'd survived out in those woods. Any number of officers could've been the one to let him know he wouldn't face charges for what he'd done, but Remi was woman enough to come herself. She deserved the same respect.

He took a step forward, unbalanced and ready to collapse. "You were right to suspend me, Remi. When I applied to the marshals, I had every intention of keeping my distance from you. You'd left Delaware for a reason, and I wasn't about to push myself back into your life if you weren't ready. Come to find out, you convinced the other division heads to send me to Oregon, and I'm glad you did."

She didn't answer, didn't even seem to breathe, apart from the slight rise of her shoulders.

He dragged a hand down his face as his legs shook. Exhaustion—mental and physical—had caught up with him, but he'd sustain another hundred stab wounds and lacerations to hang on to the short time he had with her in this room.

"I joined the marshals to finish what we started in Delaware. I thought if I could find the New Castle Killer, I could convince you to stop running from the past, to stop running from me, but what

I didn't expect was this…purpose you gave me in what we do together here. Protecting witnesses, saving lives." His chest expanded with a heavy breath, and a hint of the citrusy soap she'd used when she'd showered filled him from head to toe.

"I took that for granted, Remi, and I used a perverted version of that purpose to hunt a killer I had no jurisdiction to investigate. I know how much you rely on trusting the men and women under your command to have your back in the field. I broke that trust, and I wouldn't blame you if you felt cutting me from the team was the right thing to do." He swallowed around the ache in his throat as the reality of what his suspension meant sank in. Remi had single-handedly calmed the rage and guilt he'd carried all his life, had directed him to do something more, to be better, and he'd thrown it in her face. "I'm sorry."

He wasn't exactly sure how long he stood there, exposed and open to what came next, but he never wanted it to end. One more minute of her. That was all he needed, and he'd happily resign from USMS and pack his bags if that was what she required.

"You were hunting the New Castle Killer so I would come back to you." Disbelief tinted her words, and Remi closed the distance between them. Her body heat combined with the nervous energy clawing through him, igniting an awareness so deep, so pure, he couldn't seem to look away. "Back at the safe house, you said I was using you to relieve the stress we took on during the original investigation. If that was true, why were you so determined to find Del Howe?"

"Because I loved you then the same as I love you now." He took the risk, reaching for her. Framing her face, he hung on to her for dear life as though this was his last chance to make up for the past.

In truth, it was. Del Howe was dead. Tad Marrow was in custody. There was only Remi now. "You were more to me than the sheriff who hired me to work the investigation, just as you're more to me than my chief deputy now. You're everything I'm not, and everything I didn't know I needed in my life. You're confident, intelligent as hell, and more dangerous than anyone I've ever known because you don't rely on anyone but yourself. Except when you're getting ready to pass out from sheer exhaustion."

Her gaze narrowed on his.

"My point is, I need you, Sheriff. I need you to keep me balanced when obsession for justice gets out of control. I need you to be the example I look up to when I'm too deep into a case," he said. "I just need...you."

Her smile filled the room and rocketed his pulse into overdrive, and suddenly the pain had lost its grip. Her gaze brightened as she stepped closer to him. She reached into her pants' pocket and extracted something metallic and engraved. "Then I guess I can give you this."

His badge? Confusion warped through him and he nearly gave in to the urge to back away if it hadn't been for the addictive sensation of having her close. "I'm not a deputy anymore. You—"

"Didn't have time to file the paperwork between learning the man I fell in love with had used me and trying to keep him from dying in the middle of the woods at the hands of a psychopath we'd created together." She reached for his hand, turned it over and set the heavy metal in the center of his palm. Curling his fingers around the steel, Remi raised her gaze to his. "I didn't leave Delaware because of you, Dylan. If anything, you were the one person who made my choice all the more difficult. But I couldn't face staying in the same county I'd failed. And I didn't want to drag you down with me."

"I know." He curled his fingers around the symbol that had done more than given them each careers. It had set them on an undeniable course as friends, teammates, partners, and he'd never take this bond between them for granted again. Her words slowly registered through the last remnants of sedative and pain medication he'd needed during surgery. "Wait. I'm the man you fell in love with, right? We're not talking about Reed or Foster here."

"Nothing gets past you, Deputy Cove." She pressed her mouth to his, entangling her arms around his neck as though trying to make them one, and a backdraft of heat burned through the numbness clinging to his muscles. "You're going to wish the painkillers lasted longer after we're discharged from this place."

He deepened the kiss, healing the hollow ache in his chest that'd widened since he'd left her in that safe house.

And this time, the darkness couldn't grab hold.

This time, Remi had positioned herself between him and the void of guilt until he hardly recognized the man standing in front of her.

He'd made a mistake by not listening to Tad Marrow three years ago and failed to catch the killer responsible, but focusing on the past had been how he'd lost Remi in the first place. It was time to build the future. With the team. With her. "Believe me, Sheriff, I already do."

* * * * *

When a murder investigation reunites
Deputy Della Howard with her ex,
Sheriff Barrett Logan, she knows remaining
professional is crucial to solving this case. But as a
trained investigator, how long will it be before
Logan figures out she's carrying his child...

Keep reading for a sneak peek at
Her Child to Protect,
the first book in a brand-new series,
Mercy Ridge Lawmen, from
USA TODAY *bestselling author Delores Fossen.*

"Oh, God," she said, the words fighting with her gusting breath. "I need you to take me to the hospital now. I've been shot."

Della forced herself to slow her breathing. Panicking wouldn't help and would only make things worse. Still, it was hard to hold it together when she felt the pain stabbing through her and saw the blood.

The baby.

The fear of losing her child roared through her like an unstoppable train barreling at her. The injury wasn't that serious. Definitely not life-threatening. But any loss of blood could also mean a miscarriage.

Della nearly blurted out for Barrett to hurry, that it wasn't just her arm injury at stake, but there was no need. Barrett was already hurrying, driving as fast as he safely could, and he was doing that while on the phone with Daniel to get his brother and a team out looking for that SUV. And for the men who'd just tried to kill them.

HIEXP0421

For as long as she could remember, she'd wanted to be a cop. And wearing the badge meant facing danger just like this. But everything was different now that her baby was added to the mix. She couldn't lose his child. It didn't matter that the pregnancy hadn't been planned or that Barrett didn't want to be a father. She had to be okay so that her baby would be, too.

She managed to text Jace, to tell him that she and Barrett were heading back to the hospital and that he should do the same. Especially since Daniel would have the pursuit of the gunmen under control. Besides, she wanted Jace at the hospital in case those thugs came after Alice.

"How bad are you hurting?" Barrett asked when he ended the call with Daniel.

Della shook her head, hesitating so that she could try to get control of her voice. "It's okay."

It wasn't, of course. There was pain, but if she tried to describe it to Barrett, she might spill all about the baby. This wasn't the way she wanted him to find out. Later, after she'd been examined. Maybe after the shooters had been caught, she'd tell him then.

Thankfully, they weren't that far from the hospital, only a few minutes, and when Barrett pulled into the parking lot, he drove straight to the doors of the ER. Someone had alerted them, probably Daniel, because the moment Barrett came to a stop, a nurse and an EMT came rushing out toward them. Even though Della could have walked on her own, they put her on a gurney and rushed her into the hospital.

Barrett was right behind them.

SPECIAL EXCERPT FROM

HARLEQUIN

ROMANTIC SUSPENSE

When his nephew is taken, Jacob will do anything to get him back, even if it means accidentally kidnapping retrieval expert Norah Loblaw. Now they're working together to get Desmond back—and trying to explain their quickly growing feelings along the way.

Read on for a sneak preview of
The Negotiator,
Melinda Di Lorenzo's next thrilling romantic suspense!

He thought she deserved the full truth.

And I can't give it to her here and now.

"It's a complicated situation," he stated, hearing how weak that sounded even as he said it.

"Like Lockley?" Norah replied.

"She's a different animal completely."

The voices started up again, and Norah at last relented.

"Okay, I believe you need my help, and I'm willing to hear you out," she said. "Let's go."

Jacob didn't let himself give in to the thick relief. There was genuinely no time now. He spun on his heel and led Norah back through the slightly rank parking lot. When they reached his car, though, she stopped again.

"What are we doing?" she asked as he reached for the door handle.

HRSEXP0421

"I'd rather go over the details at my place. If you don't mind."

"You don't live here?" she asked, sounding confused.

"Here?" he echoed.

"I guess I just inferred…" She gave her head a small shake. "I'm guessing it's complicated? Again?"

He lifted his hat and scraped a hand over his hair. "You might say."

He gave the handle a tug, but Norah didn't move.

"Changing your mind?" he asked, his tone far lighter than his mind.

"No. But I need you to give me the keys," she said. "I want to drive. You can navigate."

"I thought you believed me."

"I believe you," she said mildly. "But that doesn't mean I come even close to trusting you."

Jacob nodded again, then held out the keys. As she took them, though, and he moved around to the passenger side, he realized that her words dug at him in a surprisingly forceful way. It wasn't that he didn't understand. He wouldn't have trusted himself, either, if the roles were reversed. Hell. It'd be a foolish move. It made perfect sense. But that didn't mean Jacob had to like it.